C000068108

THE LOST RING

Kathy Farmer

authorHOUSE®

AuthorHouse™ UK Ltd.
1663 Liberty Drive
Bloomington, IN 47403 USA
www.authorhouse.co.uk
Phone: 0800.197.4150

© 2014 Kathy Farmer. All rights reserved.

No part of this book may be reproduced, stored in a retrieval system, or transmitted by any means without the written permission of the author.

Published by AuthorHouse 08/27/2014

ISBN: 978-1-4969-8922-2 (sc)
ISBN: 978-1-4969-8923-9 (e)

Any people depicted in stock imagery provided by Thinkstock are models, and such images are being used for illustrative purposes only. Certain stock imagery © Thinkstock.

This book is printed on acid-free paper.

Because of the dynamic nature of the Internet, any web addresses or links contained in this book may have changed since publication and may no longer be valid. The views expressed in this work are solely those of the author and do not necessarily reflect the views of the publisher, and the publisher hereby disclaims any responsibility for them.

Knighton 22nd October.
To my dear friend Maggie.
With love and every blessing.
Kathy

I dedicate this book to my children –
Jonathan and Julia

PROLOGUE

BALMORAL 1864

Today was glorious as we rode along the peaty paths on our highland ponies, The scenery was grand and wild as we made our way along a narrow pass between the mountains, until the head of a Glen widened as Loch Lee came into view, closed in by the mountains. We dismounted and stopped for a light luncheon at the shooting lodge.

As I entered, the pipers struck up. I felt very moved. The last time I had come here was with my dearest one. I never thought that it was to be the last time. I felt as though I could not face life without him and had shut myself away for a long time in my grief, but Brown, my late husband's ghillie, rescued me and has given me back a zest for life and I find myself enjoying the beauty of this journey. I think I was taken aback by Brown at first. He was respectful but with none of the deferential humbug of a servant and yet the man loves me as his Sovereign, just as he loved and served my dearest Albert..

Two of my ladies and an equerry make up our party, with Brown looking after the ponies and the dog-cart, should I get tired. When he rides beside me we chat together quite naturally and he points out many interesting things of nature to me. This afternoon I shall go down to the loch to sketch.

*   *   *

At dinner tonight my hand automatically went to caress the mourning ring I had had made by my jewellers after Albert's death and which I wore on my little finger. It wasn't there! I felt so distressed that I left the table and went to my room. It was nowhere to be found. It has slipped off my finger, perhaps when I became so cold sketching this afternoon down by the loch, maybe into a clump of heather, or into the marshy ground beside the loch?---------I fear that I shall never know.

CHAPTER ONE

2009

Vicky was met at Aberdeen airport by her son Bruce. It was their first meeting since the funeral of his father and they were both a little emotional. She had expected his wife Lindsay to be with him. but he excused her absence saying that she was very busy with her market garden business.

Bruce was tall and dark, just like his father Vicky thought with a pang as he helped her into his car. Her husband Ian's death had been sudden and unexpected. He was only in his fifties and like most farmers appeared fit and healthy He had suffered a heart attack out in one of the barns and had been unable to summon help. Vicky had been distraught. She had loved him dearly. They had married young and worked together as one in all aspects of their farming life.

It had always been something of a disappointment to them both, when Bruce showed a disinclination to farm after University where, he had met and later married a Scots lass and moved to Scotland to start a publishing business in Edinburgh. It had been a sadness to them both to realise that the farm they had both worked so hard for. would not be passed on down the family in due time, and where they could also have enjoyed an on-going interest in the farm, living nearby in a cottage perhaps and watch their grand-children grow up. Instead, it had meant that they didn't

1

see each other as much as they would have liked, with all their commitments of farming and the travelling distance involved. Oh, why had they let so much time slip by without seeing each other more often, she thought, before it was too late. If only they had known it was all going to end so soon. She knew that Bruce was suffering over the death of his father and would feel the regret of lost times.

At the funeral he and Lindsay had been helpful and supportive as had her daughter, Jane, who now lived in London with her husband and their two boys. Both wanted her to come and stay with them but for several months she had put them off. There was so much business to see to and decisions to be made as to what she did with the farm. She had offered Bruce the option of the farm, but he had declined it. He had been out of farming too long and had made his home in Scotland with Lindsay and their son Callum. His publishing business was getting established. She understood but nevertheless had felt a little sad.

It was only now, on the threshold of selling up that she felt able to take some time to visit. She was anxious to see her grandson Callum, but of course he would be at school now, she thought, looking at her watch. Bruce said, "I've taken some time off mum, so that we can do things together."

"Thank you Bruce, that's very good of you, I appreciate it. How is the business dear?" she asked.

"Well, recession is really beginning to bite with banks and firms going belly-up, just hope that we can weather it, mum, nobody knows really."

They left the main road and took a narrow lane up one of the glens, the mountains rose before her in all their grandeur. They turned off the lane onto a rough track which led to The Croft. Bruce didn't have a lot of land but he liked to keep a few sheep to keep it tidy and to give sufficient grazing for Lindsay's horse. Bruce nosed the car into the shelter of the stone house, stables and barns which made a sheltered L shape. Bruce helped her out and took her case but Vicky stood rapt at the riot of colour that dazzled the eye as it leapt from the boxes and pots of flowers and shrubs, to trays of different hues of heather in front of the barns. This would be Lindsay's new market-garden business, Vicky thought. Well, it was all very industrious of her daughter-in-law and she mentally took her hat off to her. Good old Lindsay!

Hamish, their black Labrador gun dog came over to greet her, tail happily swinging from side to side. Bruce had gone into the house before her and was putting the kettle on for tea. He took her case into her bedroom on the ground floor just off the kitchen. It had been a self-contained flat for a housekeeper, now it was ideal for a guest. They went back into the kitchen for a cup of tea. After a little while Lindsay came in dressed in dungarees, She held earthy hands up as she kicked her wellies off and went over to the sink first to wash her hands. She turned her head,

"Hello Vicky, please excuse me I'm so dirty, be with you in a minute." Turning the tap off she wiped her hands on a towel, wriggled out of her dungarees before coming to embrace her mother-in-law. Lindsay was tall and slender. She had blue eyes, short dark curly hair framed a fresh complexioned face. Her mouth was lusciously plump. When Vicky and her husband had first known her she had seemed like an exuberant puppy, in love with their son and anxious to please.

Vicky and Lindsay shared an interest in common, and that was their love of horses. When Lindsay and Bruce had visited them, Vicky had always borrowed a horse for her and they would ride out together through one of the many tracts of forestry where they lived. She had always felt how lucky she was to have a daughter-in-law with whom she could share a mutual interest. It was only later that Vicky had been somewhat dismayed when, after their baby grandson Callum, was born, Lindsay didn't seem able to cope, either with the baby or with housework, great piles of ironing would accumulate. Mealtimes were ignored to the point of starvation, and worse still, Callum was left to his own devices, neglected she thought, while Lindsay attended to her horses or her pots and plants. It was not a comfortable house where she and Ian had felt wanted when they visited and so they had stopped going, giving the excuse that they couldn't leave the farm, but Vicky knew that had things been different, she would have made the time to go and see her grandson. Bruce put his mug down on the table, and stood up. "I'll go and meet Callum off the school bus."

"Did you have a good flight?" Lindsay asked, without looking at her as she switched the television on.

"There was an awful lot of turbulence, taking off and landing but it got me here so quickly, without the hassle of driving. I enjoyed it. I caught sight of your mare in the field, do you ride her much now that you have the plant business?"

"No, not a lot. I haven't the time. Did you bring jods. and boots?" Vicky nodded.

"I've got a spare hat you can borrow."

"Have you got a spare horse for me to ride?" she asked. Then you could come out with me, stop me from getting lost."

"I'm too busy, Vicky. I don't have the time. The Gilchrists breed Highland ponies. I could maybe get you one that's been schooled and we'll keep it here for you to ride whenever you want. I'll see Andrew, the son tomorrow." She had a good heart, Vicky thought. She perhaps took too

4

much on with a youngster, livestock and now her market garden business to look after. Perhaps I've been too critical of her, Vicky thought. Just then Bruce came through the door with Callum. Vicky opened her arms to him. And he ran into them. "Hello, grandma," he said rolling his R's like the born and bred Scots boy he was. He was eight, dark haired with big brown eyes.

"There's a parcel on my bed," Vicky said. "Would you like to go and get it for me?" he ran to do her bidding and came back with it.

"There you are" she said putting it back in his arms, "It's for you. Go on, open it."

"Thank you grandma," he said serious faced as he tore at the paper. He uncovered an adventure book. He fingered the cover which showed a boy and a wolf in a wild background of range and forests. She had chosen it because she had always been fascinated by wolves, and she hoped he too would like an adventure story about them. Carefully he unfolded another parcel. It was a fishing gilet with lots of pockets for keeping flies and other bits and pieces in, just like his dad wore and then there was a really nice pocket knife, useful for making a bow and arrows, he thought. He was really pleased and threw his arms around Vicky.

"Thank you, grandma."

"My pleasure," she said, and meant it. Callum was a totally unspoilt boy and she knew that he was genuinely pleased with her gifts. He ran upstairs to take his school uniform off and put the fishing gilet on, he slipped the knife into one of its many pockets.

"What are we having for dinner tonight?" Bruce asked Lindsay. She went over to the fridge and opened the door. Peering in she murmured,

"--we might not have enough mince for Bolognese---"

"Oh, for goodness sake there's plenty of game in the freezer, trout, venison, duck, pheasant." Bruce said with ill concealed exasperation.

"Oh, I think there will be enough mince," she said, taking it out, ignoring Bruce. Vicky sensed her son's irritation at his wife's lack of preparation for her visit and was embarrassed.

Vicky excused herself and went to her room to freshen up after the journey. One tiny hand towel had been put out for her. Oh dear, she would have to ask for a bath towel, she couldn't manage with this for a week. It was just Lindsay, she didn't think.

Several hours later they all sat down around the kitchen table for a rather skimpy spaghetti Bolognese. Lindsay had her eyes glued to the television throughout, and conversation died. Now and again she would laugh out loud at something that had amused her on the box. Homework was non-existent and bedtime for Callum was when he dropped with weariness.

Vicky went upstairs with Bruce who took him to bed. and she read to him from the new book she had bought, before kissing him goodnight.

"Love you lots" she said.

"I love you too grandma," he replied in his serious way.

By now Vicky was exhausted. Returning to the kitchen she noticed the washing-up had not been done and set to, stacking the dishes in the drainer before saying goodnight, leaving Lindsay smoking and still watching tv. Baskets of ironing waiting to be done had not escaped her notice. She felt that the rest of her time here was going to be something of an endurance test. She asked Bruce to get her a bath towel.

The next morning she and Callum were the first ones up, he was shaking cornflakes into his bowl. He stood uncertainly, proffering the box.

"Do you want some grandma?"

"Perhaps I'd better wait for your mummy and daddy."

"Mum's still in bed," he volunteered just as Bruce appeared who went to a cupboard and got plates and a bowl for them, a jug of milk, butter and marmalade. He put some bread in the toaster.

"Lindsay's going to jump Jet in a show near Aberdeen today, you'll like that won't you mum?" She thought back to the times when she had risen very early to get her horses ready to show. They were shampooed, dried, brushed until they shone, manes plaited, tails untangled and left silky. The night before, all the tack had been taken apart, cleaned with saddle soap and left to dry whilst she polished buckles and stirrups and then a final duster over the saddles and bridles, re-assembled everything. How on earth was Lindsay going to achieve all this when she was still in bed?

"Is there anything I can do to help her get Jet ready?" she asked Bruce.

"Oh no you don't," said Lindsay just coming through the door. "I do my own mare, thank you."

Vicky felt snubbed. Lindsay was so off-hand with her she instinctively felt unwanted. Her son Bruce, was in a difficult position, she knew. He was in the middle, between his wife and his mother, even if he said something it would not help. These were the times when she missed her husband and the closeness they had shared. She could almost hear him say, Why did you come, you knew what it would be like? and she was sad that he too had been made to feel unwanted.

7

"If you really want to help you could do some ironing for me." Vicky bit back the words that rose in her head. She didn't answer, pretending not to hear her but went outside and found Callum to talk to. He had let Hamish out of his kennel and was throwing a stick for him to retrieve. Bruce was manoeuvering the horse-box into position in the yard ready to take the mare. Vicky had to admit that Lindsay had worked hard on Jet, her black coat was gleaming with a blue sheen, as she stood ready to be loaded. Various brushes, a bucket and a net of hay was put in the back. After disappearing into the house Lindsay appeared immaculately dressed in jodhpurs, boots, shirt and stock and black riding jacket. She carried her hat. "Right, we're ready to go then. The box will only take the three of us in the front, you won't mind following us in our car, will you?" she said holding out the keys to Vicky.

"I'll come with you, grandma." Callum offered. As the horsebox trundled its way slowly, she followed behind with Callum who gave her a running commentary on where to turn.

"Would you like a pony of your own?" she asked him.

"No way," he said emphatically. "They run away with you." It was obvious that he had had a bad experience that had put him off.

The ground was large and because there was a cold wind blowing off the sea, Vicky thought that it was too cold for her and Callum to stand around whilst Lindsay tacked the mare up and exercised her to warm her up for her class, so they left Bruce to help Lindsay, whilst they walked around the other rings and trade stalls. After a while she looked at her watch and thought they had better make their way back to where Lindsay and Bruce were. Passing a horsebox she saw Morag, Lindsay's close friend, tacking up her chestnut hunter. "Hello Morag, Your horse looks in tiptop condition," she said stroking the chestnut's nose "Are you competing in the same class as Lindsay?" Morag looked at her as though she had never seen her before.

"I'm Callum's grandmother, remember?" she prompted, with a smile.

"Oh,-- yes, hello." Morag said, but without any enthusiasm. How strange, Vicky thought, as they moved away, she seemed almost unfriendly. Callum piped up as though he read her thoughts.

"They're not friends any more."

"Oh,---- why?"

"I don't know," he said skipping beside her.

They went to join Bruce at the ringside. They could see Lindsay on Jet waiting for the class to start. The first round went very well for her, and she jumped it faultlessly. In the next jump-off the mare had gone clear until they approached a triple jump. The mare's stride was all wrong as she approached it. Vicky heard Bruce gasp. Jet saw her mistake and tried desperately to clear the pole before she brought the first one down and then crashed awkwardly, legs straddled between the next two poles. For a moment it looked as though Lindsay was going to have a bad fall, as the mare gallantly struggled out of the debris of fallen poles. She heard Bruce's sudden intake of breath and he went white but somehow Lindsay hung on and regained her seat. She was eliminated. They trotted out of the ring. Lindsay popped Jet over a few practice fences to restore the mare's confidence, before taking her back and tying her up to the side of the horsebox to wait for her other classes. She joined them at the ringside.

"Oh my Goodness, you gave us a fright," Bruce said to Lindsay as she joined them. "I know, I just couldn't get her right."

"You were lucky you didn't come off." Vicky, who had done it all before, when she was young like Lindsay thought, *what a hell of a risk to take when you have a young family,*

"You did very well dear, after all she is still a young novice and she has a lot to learn."

"I know, I haven't got the time now to school her." They watched to see the end of the class and saw Morag take the cup, neither Lindsay nor Bruce made any comment. Vicky thought it very strange and wondered what had come between them. In the next class Jet had some refusals and it was obvious that her earlier mistake was still with her and that the mare was unsettled. Lindsay was wise to call it a day. They watched some dressage before packing up to go home.

Once home, Lindsay was quite happy to leave Jet in her mother-in-law's care. She went into the house to change out of her show gear. Vicky brushed the dried-on sweat off the mare, she had a way with horses, making little shushing noises as she brushed, which soothed and relaxed them. She fed the mare and tied up a net of hay for her. As she worked, she hoped that Lindsay was getting a meal for them, she was starving. But it was Bruce who was preparing trout with Callum's help, for dinner. Lindsay was smoking. She looked up from watching tv as Vicky came in,

"Thank you, for feeding Jet and bedding her down, I'm absolutely bushed."

After dinner, Callum was told by his father to go and get his uniform ready to put on in the morning for scout parade at the kirk, and to clean his shoes and have a shower before he went to bed. grandma was coming to see him on parade!

*　　*　　*

Bruce drove Vicky and Callum to the village kirk. As they got out of the car into the spring sunshine, Callum ran to join his friends waiting to line up for their parade once the rest of the congregation had gone in. The kirk was packed with parents and grandparents. Vicky recognized some of Bruce and Lindsay's neighbours and they nodded and smiled back at her. As they took their seats Vicky asked Bruce, whether Lindsay ever came to the kirk with them.

"No," he said shortly, making it obvious he didn't want any more questions. Nevertheless, she couldn't help wondering if Callum was upset by the absence of his mother when he saw his friends' parents come to see them. She hadn't seen Lindsay this morning and presumed that she was still in bed when they left.

The service started with the brownies and girl guides parading down the aisle followed by the cubs and scouts following the standard-bearers. As Callum passed them he gave her a broad grin. The children with their leaders took their seats and went up to receive their prizes for the examinations they had passed in their various skills. Some children read the Lesson, and after the service they received the standard and paraded out. It was a proud day for parents and children to come together in the kirk once a month, surely not too much to ask of Lindsay, Vicky couldn't help thinking.

Outside the kirk, Vicky saw Jean Ferguson who had been recently widowed, like herself. She too had come to see her grandchildren in the parade. "It's so good to see you. How long are you here for?" Jean asked her.

"Oh, I'm only here for the week."

"Then you must come and have tea with me this week. How about Tuesday afternoon?"

"Thank you Jean, that would be lovely." Just then Callum found them, Jean had a soft spot for him and told him how smart he had looked in the parade. They both examined his new badges.

"Don't forget, next Tuesday." Jean waved at her as they started to go back to their cars with their families.

Back at the Croft, Lindsay was nowhere to be found. Bruce got on with the dinner. He put a haunch of venison on whilst she prepared the vegetables. "Where do you think she's gone?" Vicky asked him.

"Oh, I don't know. She could be lost in the potting shed or out on Jet or visiting a friend. She'll be back in a minute, I'm sure."

Callum piped up," Mummy's not out on Jet, she's in her field. I'll go and look for her.""Change out of your uniform first." Bruce ordered him. Callum groaned and pulled a face as he dragged himself upstairs. Vicky laid the table. The feeling grew stronger that something was not right here. Bruce was carving the joint when Lindsay appeared. She breezed in smiling, not a care in the world,

"Oh, good. she said, I'm really hungry, and it smells marvellous."

"Where have you been, all this time?" Bruce asked.

"I went over to the Gilchrists to see Andrew about getting a Highland pony, for Vicky to be able to trek on whilst she's here."

"Oh, what did he say?"

"He'll bring one round today or tomorrow for Vicky to try." Bruce laughed, "They can be canny little devils sometimes mum, I've seen Lindsay come off them." he warned.

"Och, that's only when I've been breaking one in for him." Lindsay said. Andrew Gilchrist came that evening leading a grey Highland pony called Tweed, whose forelock hung down like dreadlocks so thick and long that it covered his eyes. His mane too hung down in a thick profusion of ringlets. Jet came galloping across the field to see him. She screamed a high-pitched whinny of excitement but Tweed remained stolidly calm. They stabled him to let him and Jet get acquainted slowly before they put them together in the field, in case they kicked or bit each other.

"We'll let them both calm down before I try him out," Vicky said. Andrew left her Tweed's saddle and bridle.

"My mother is looking forward to seeing you," he told Vicky,

"I will come and see Beth before I go back home," she promised. Callum stroked Tweed's nose. He thought that the pony didn't look as dangerous as Jet. In fact, he thought when he and grandma were alone he too might climb on Tweed's back. It was a pity he had to go to school tomorrow.

* * *

CHAPTER TWO

"I thought that I would take you up one of the other glens this morning mum, there's a beautiful loch there I would love you to see. The mountains rise up all around it. We could do a bit of fishing, I'll hire a boat and take my outboard motor and we can take a picnic and some coffee.. What do you think?"

"It sounds lovely. Will Lindsay be coming?" she asked. Bruce shook his head, "No, she's getting all her plants and shrubs ready to take to a market today, and we don't have to be back until it's time to meet Callum off the school bus. So the day is ours."

The loch was situated some miles northwest in a deeply wooded glen.

"This adjoins part of the Balmoral Estate, "he told her. "In fact the loch is closed to the general public except for a few times in the year, which happens to be today for us, so we are lucky. Royalty and their visitors, ever since Queen Victoria's day have fished the loch and had shoots here. when they are in residence."

Vicky looked around her as Bruce pointed out the shooting lodge and where there had once stood an old castle, its crumbling stonework now festooned in ivy. They parked the car and walked down to the loch and the boathouse. It was just as he had described it, stunningly beautiful with the loch closed in by mountains which seemed to rise straight out of the water.

Bruce fitted his outboard onto the back of the boat, loaded their fishing tackle safely and helped her climb in. He pull-started the motor and it roared into life. They puttered across the loch until they were in the middle. There was not another soul about. Bruce suggested that before they started fly-fishing proper, he should teach his mother dapping, gently touching the surface of the water with the moving fly. She soon got the hang of it and to her amazement she felt a tug on the line and had hooked a trout. Bruce didn't think it was big enough and put it back. They fly-fished for another two hours. She had no luck but Bruce had caught a couple of fine trout for supper. After a little while they decided to picnic on the wilder opposite shore where there was no path or road along the loch. They beached the boat safely up onto the sandy shale at the edge of the water.

As they ate their sandwiches he told her that this was the home of the golden eagle, the merlin and osprey. On occasions he had been privileged to see them all. Everything in nature interested him. Vicky wondered how he reconciled this interest with his prowess with the gun. It was a dilemma of conscience that warred with the naturalist and the old hunting instinct of man. She poured them both a steaming hot coffee from the flask and stood up. She was stiff from too much sitting. Age was catching up, she thought ruefully. Although, in her early fifties, she liked to think that she could still lead the active life she had always had when she and Ian had farmed together and welcomed Bruce's suggestion when he asked, "Would you like me to take you over to the other side mum, so that you can have a walk? There's a path along the loch, I've got a map that you can have and I'll carry on fishing until you return." He took her over to the other side and steered the boat into a little opening between large boulders. "I'll stay in the middle of the loch and I'll come and pick you up here when you come back." He helped her out of the boat. "Take as long as you like mum. There's no hurry," and with a wave he was off back across the loch.

Oh, what a relief to be able to stretch her limbs and walk off the numbing stiffness, she thought. Vicky consulted the map. It showed that there were several footpaths that she could choose to follow when she got to the head of the loch. She folded the map up and stuffed it into her Barbour. She had felt a little chilly in the boat. It would be good to have a brisk walk. There had been a mist first thing hanging over the water and the mountains but now the sun had come out and dispelled the mist revealing the grandeur of the craggy tops of the mountains. It was getting hot. As she walked, she gloried in the lush greenness about her. Waterfalls roared as they tumbled and frothed white over boulders into pristine rushing streams. Everything looked fresh and shining. If only she could be sharing this beauty with her husband. She was grateful for her children, Bruce, inviting her to stay with him and Lindsay in Scotland and when she returned, she had promised Jane, her daughter, to go and stay with her and her husband Mark and their two boys in London. That would be a contrast, she thought. She understood that they were all trying to be supportive and kind to her but she felt so terribly the odd one out and in a way all she wanted was to be left alone. It was lovely to see her son and grandson Callum, of course, but she was ill at ease with an indefinable feeling that all was not well between Bruce and Lindsay, which left her with a feeling of anxiety. There was no one for her to confide in. She felt her aloneness all the more.

Vicky came to the head of the loch. A path snaked endlessly before her down the valley for miles skirting the mountains on either side and disappearing into the blue mistiness of a forest in the far distance, a little like my life now, she thought bleakly and turned to follow the path to her right which went uphill and twisted and turned so that she couldn't see where it would take her. After toiling up a steep incline and still not reaching its summit, she felt breathless and sat on a boulder to rest beside a rushing burn. She looked at her watch. Perhaps she had better be starting back, although she would have liked to reach the end of this path snaking ever upward, for there might be a fine view once she had reached the top.

Suddenly she heard a man's voice singing. It came to her in little snatches at first, carried on the breeze, getting louder until gradually over the rise of the hill, a man appeared walking toward her with a long thumb-stick in his hand. He stopped singing when he saw her and grinned rather sheepishly as he drew alongside. He wore a dark sweater with a brightly coloured kerchief around his neck. His hair was dark and swept back. It sprang into little curls around his neck. Clear blue eyes looked at her out of a tanned rugged face that suggested he led an outdoor life. He smiled with embarrassment. "Hello, I thought I was all alone, please excuse me, but it's such a marvellous day," spreading his arms to embrace the mountains and the sky.

"Not at all, you're quite right, it is wonderful." She stood up to walk back, "I'm walking back to meet my son down by the loch."

"Oh, I'm going back that way too, Shall we walk together? "he extended his hand," John Brown"

Vicky's eyebrows lifted, "Not, *The* John Brown?" and they both laughed.

"Well, I think I could be distantly related."

"Vicky Lewis," she responded withdrawing her hand from his, as they fell into step together. At this he stopped and faced her,

"*Not Vicky as in Queen Victoria?*" It was her turn to laugh.

"Yes, John Brown, but I don't think that I am even distantly related.

Do you live here?" she asked.

"Yes, I do. What about you?"

"I've come to visit my son and family who live up one of the other glens,"

"Which one?" he asked.

"Clova."

"Good Lord !" he exclaimed, "My place is up there. What a coincidence."

"Please don't tell me that you are a ghillie to the Royal family?" He shook his head, "There, now the spell is broken." he laughed. "Although I could turn my hand to that too." He found himself instinctively liking this woman with her sense of humour which lit up her large dark eyes out of a pale oval face. Her hair was straight and dark except for a little quiff of grey which made her look rather stylish, he thought. It seemed to him that it had been a long time since he had last laughed

They chatted amicably, almost like old friends until they came to the head of the loch. Vicky stopped and pointed to the boat out in the middle of the loch where Bruce was still casting. She waved to him and he waved back.

"Well, since we are almost neighbours, I may see you again Ma'am." he said with a mock bow. Vicky smiled. "Goodbye John Brown."

She started to make her way down to the bit of a slipway between the boulders. Bruce put his rod in the boat, started the engine and puttered over to pick her up. He got out of the boat and stepped into the water to help her in. "Who was that?" he asked her, his eye on the receding figure of John Brown walking along the side of the loch.

"I just met him walking and singing,---- he lives here, up our glen. He introduced himself as John Brown."

"--as John Brown?" he said quizzically. "Oh mother, do be careful."

"He was very nice," she said remembering how sympathetic he had been when she told him of her husband's death. Perhaps she shouldn't have told that to a complete stranger. Maybe it was her loneliness that had made her confide in him. He had responded by telling her that he too had lost his wife and how hard the adjustment was without her. It had been good to speak with someone who understood. Anyway she was unlikely to ever see him again.

Bruce was just about to get back into the boat when something caught his eye under the shelved waterline. He bent and picked it up out of the sandy silt, looked at it briefly and then threw it into her lap. "Here you are mum. It looks as though someone has lost their ring," as he pushed the boat out from the shallows, jumped in and started the motor. "I think we'll make our way back up to the boathouse now."

Vicky looked at the ring. A cheap little thing, she thought. It seemed to be covered in rust. She would throw it back into the loch. Idly she scratched at it and bright gold gleamed back at her. She continued to scratch. A double coil of gold was revealed that twisted into a Celtic love-knot on either side of a small bloodstone. It felt rough in places and she gasped with astonishment as a small crown gradually appeared deeply engraved into the bloodstone with a scrolled letter 'A', under it.

"No one wears a ring with a crown on it ----unless they are royalty" she said haltingly with awe in her voice to Bruce. "I wonder if it was a gift from Albert signifying their love, or maybe a mourning ring of Queen Victoria's to remind her of Albert. After all, they did come here, on their ponies to this very loch.-----or maybe, later, when she travelled this way again with John Brown. Maybe the Queen dabbled her fingers in the water after a picnic and it fell off her little finger," she said excitedly. "It's very small, it will only fit my little finger. "Look," she showed him. "If I washed my hands it would easily fall off.----It could be very valuable.--- Do we have to tell anyone?---- Is it treasure trove?"

"No, it's not treasure trove if it has been lost, only if it has been hidden deliberately for some reason. Don't tell Lindsay, that I found it," he suddenly warned. "I want you to have it." By this time they had reached the boathouse. She picked up their things and carried them out of the boat whilst Bruce took the outboard motor off. He stopped to speak to a ghillie before catching her up to walk back to the car. They stowed their things in the boot. Once in the car he studied the ring. It needed cleaning properly, but he could see how unusual and beautiful it was.

"You found it," Vicky said, "it's yours really but I'll keep it for you, if you like, but why must it be kept a secret from Lindsay?"

"Because I want you to have it mum. Please tell her that you found it. I would only have chucked it back into the loch. It looked so awful."

Vicky was not sure that she was convinced by what he said, He held the ring out for her to take and she put it on her little finger and then feeling that it could slip off, she zipped it into a pocket.

"You know," she said, "When I'm back in London visiting Jane and Mark, I could take it to the Victoria and Albert museum to see if I can find out a little more about it."

"Yes, that might be a good idea."

At breakfast the next morning Lindsay said that she was going to see her sister and would be back some time mid-afternoon. Bruce asked Vicky whether she would like to pop into town with him, he had some business there to attend to, after he had seen Callum safely on the school bus.

"No, my dear. I shall ride Tweed this morning and then I am taking tea with Jean Ferguson this afternoon, so I have a full day planned for myself. I shall be quite happy doing my own thing." she said with a smile at them both.

Later, as she brushed Tweed, she felt that it was almost a relief to be on her own. She tried to tuck his voluminous forelock up into the brow-band of the bridle so that he could see where he was going but decided that he looked more noble with it hanging across his eyes and half-way down his nose. With the horse saddled up and girth tightened, she eased herself into the saddle. He stood solidly patient, until she moved him on.

Jet, Lindsay's mare, wanted to come with them and screamed and whinnied after them until they were out of sight. Even this left Tweed unmoved. He was a willing little horse, and after walking she tried his other paces. He didn't appear to have any of the devilment in him that Bruce had warned her about, even when the odd car raced inconsiderately past them. They entered some woods and cantered along the paths until she could see the top a large grey stone house. A harsh cry startled them both and the pony tensed under her, ready to bolt.

"Steady now," she soothed Tweed as she looked around her. From the back of the pony she could see over the box clipped yew hedge surrounding the gardens of the house. She could see a large caged enclosure. A hawk flew across emitting the same harsh cry of warning. She turned Tweed around to walk back. Surely, she thought, it was illegal to keep any bird of prey in captivity. She would ask Bruce if he knew who lived there.

*   *   *

Jean Ferguson had only recently moved to a smaller house after her husband Jim's death. Before, they had farmed and lived in an old rambling house, not far from The Croft. As Vicky and Jean took tea together, Vicky recalled how she had first met them when she had taken a short-cut back to Bruce and Lindsay's place after a walk. The path had taken her through the Ferguson's farmyard where someone had wolf-whistled her. She had looked around but could see no one. Feeling decidedly uneasy and embarrassed she had hurried back to the Croft with the wolf-whistles following her until she was out of earshot and sight of the perpetrator. When she told Bruce about her experience he had fallen about laughing, "Oh, that's Jim's African Grey parrot. If it's a nice day they hang his cage from a tree outside where he wolf-whistles anyone who passes."

"I was so relieved when I knew it was the parrot." she told Jean, laughing. Now, the farm, land, horses and parrot had gone and they talked together in Jean's new bungalow, with understanding and empathy as only they could, about the changes that they had had to make to their lives as they contemplated life without their husbands beside them. It was a hard upward struggle of adjustment which Vicky too had had to make, with just the contract to sign in selling their hill farm in Wales. Vicky had found all this heart-breaking.

Her home where her children had been born and which held so many happy memories for her was now ended. Jean pointed out that at least they had their family as a comfort. They fell silent and then Jean remarked rather artlessly,

"It's such a shame that Lindsay doesn't ever come to the kirk with Bruce, or to see Callum on scout parade. I never see the girl and I feel sorry for your Bruce too. It's a pity you live so far away. Maybe you'll come and live here?" she said with an enquiring smile.

"Oh, I don't know, mothers and daughters- in- laws are better kept apart." Vicky said lightly.

"Your Bruce is such a nice young man---Jim was very fond of him. I hope he is happy." Alarm bells began to ring for Vicky. It was as though Jean knew something that she didn't and was trying to warn her. She changed the subject.

"I'm going to see Beth Gilchrist tomorrow for coffee. I've borrowed one of their Highland ponies while I'm here. I'll probably ride him over there. He's nice and steady. I rode up the glen on him this morning and through that woodland a mile or two on and came to this big house where there were birds of prey in an enclosure. Do you know who lives there?" she asked Jean.

"I don't really know, Jim knew about him. He used to call on him, about fishing, I think. He called him 'the Professor.' Other people call him, the Laird." Vicky gave a sigh of relief, "Oh good, I thought that I had stumbled across something illegal, going on." She put her tea-cup on the tray. "I'm going back to Wales in a few days and then I shall drive to London to stay with my daughter for a while Jean, and I probably won't be up for another year, but it's been lovely to see you again and have a chat."

"And you," said Jean, giving her a hug.

23

*   *   *

That evening after tea Vicky asked Callum if he would like to ride Tweed if she led him on a halter?

"Oh, yes please." he said. He liked the look of Tweed, he didn't look as though he would run away with him. Vicky raised a questioning glance at Lindsay for permission. She was glued to the television, but she must have heard and briefly turned her head and nodded. They went out like two conspirators together. Callum brushed him for awhile before grandma popped him up on his nice broad back and led him around in circles on a long rein. At first they walked this way and that and then grandma clicked him into a trot which made Callum hang on to his long mane. He felt like a sack of potatoes. It wasn't at all comfortable. Then they walked up the long drive and back. Hamish, the labrador went with them. Back home grandma praised his first lesson on Tweed. He had to give him another brush before turning him out into the field with Jet. It had been fun and he had fallen in love withTweed.

CHAPTER THREE

Vicky rode Tweed over to the Gilchrists farm the next morning to see Beth. Andrew, her son, saw her coming and went over to meet her, wondering if she was bringing Tweed back because he was unsuitable.

"Good heavens, no! He's a wonderful pony. I've come over to see your mother, and I knew that you could pop him into one of your stables until I'm ready to go back. In fact, I would quite like to buy him." Andrew grinned with relief, "Would it be for yourself or for young Callum.?" he enquired.

"Oh, Callum, of course, but I need to ask his mother first. How much would Tweed cost?"

"I'll consult dad, we'll see what we can do for you." he led Tweed away while Vicky made her way to the back door of the farmhouse. Beth came to meet her. She was older than Vicky and had kept a motherly eye on Bruce when he lived alone in a bungalow before he married Lindsay.

"How are you, my dear? Ivor and I were so sorry to hear of your husband's death." Coffee and biscuits were laid out on the farmhouse table and Beth clucked over her as she handed Vicky her coffee. She sat down opposite her and studied her with an interested sympathy so that Vicky bit her lip hard and hoped she wasn't going to dissolve into tears. She didn't feel quite so comfortable with Beth as she felt with Jean.

"How long are you staying?" she asked her.

"I'm going to stay with my daughter the following week. Oh Beth, it's been lovely to see Callum, he's such a lovely boy, so undemanding, plays quite happily by himself. I suppose it's because he's an only child."

"How are you getting on with Lindsay?" Beth asked rather pointedly. Vicky smiled, she knew that Beth and Lindsay didn't much like each other

"Lindsay is Lindsay. She is very occupied with her market garden business. I've hardly seen anything of her."

"Have you seen Morag, her friend?"

Vicky thought. "I saw her compete at a show near Aberdeen, but I haven't really seen her to talk to."

"Don't they ride out together any more?"

"Well, I haven't seen them. In fact Lindsay seems too busy to ride. Why do you ask?" Beth shrugged her shoulders, "There's a rumour that they are no longer friends".

"Oh?" Vicky said and wondered where she had heard it and then remembered, it had come from Callum. (Out of the mouths of babes!)

"They say," said Beth confidingly, "that Lindsay and Morag's husband were getting too close." As she delivered the death-blow, Vicky knew why she preferred her friend Jean to this woman who had gossiping troublemaker written all over her. The biscuit stuck in her throat and she felt sick.

"I've always said, your Bruce is too good for her. He probably doesn't know what's been going on."

Vicky downed her coffee and said that she must be going. Bruce was going to drive her into town this afternoon. She thanked Beth for the coffee and with a wave hurried over to the stable block to get Tweed and make her escape. She was shaking. She had known something was wrong and now it had just been confirmed. What was she to do? Maybe it had all blown over. If that was so, Bruce would not like to know that she knew. She hurried back.

Bruce was in the kitchen when she returned, making them a sandwich for lunch. "How did your morning with Beth go?" he asked. "I must say, although she has been very good to me in the past, Lindsay can't stand her, she calls her an interfering old biddy. For some reason Beth is very critical of her, probably jealous of her life-style with her horse and plant business, not the typical farmer's wife."

"No." Vicky murmured, and then couldn't help asking.

"Is everything alright between you and Lindsay?" He looked up. "Oh come on, what's Beth been saying?"

"What's happened between Morag and Lindsay?"

"Oh, so that's it." he laughed. "Morag thought that Graham, her husband was spending too much time with Lindsay in the potting shed. They both help each other out with their market-garden business, you see." He shrugged, "Maybe he was a bit sweet on her, I've seen them sitting with their heads together potting the seedlings, but I think Graham was playing away from home with someone else. Morag had the cheek to wake us up in the middle of the night demanding that Lindsay send Graham home. We had been in bed for hours. Well, after that, Lindsay had nothing more to do with them. End of story."

"So,----- everything is alright between you? You still love her?"

"Yes. Lindsay's a lovely girl mum." he said, frowning, obviously ruffled by what she had suggested.

"Good." She remembered how white his face had been when he thought Lindsay was going to have a bad fall at the show. He still loved her, despite her slip-shod ways in the home, but was he being taken for a fool? Did Lindsay still love him? She always seemed so critical and derisory when she spoke of him. But Bruce had defended her and despite her misgivings she must accept what he had said. Clearly he was not worried, even though alarm bells still rang for her.

"I might as well tell you now mum, although Lindsay wanted to wait awhile before telling you-----" Vicky looked up, "Tell me, what?"

"Lindsay's pregnant. You're going to have another grandchild." Bruce had always teased her about them not having another child saying that it didn't fit in with his shooting season or the fishing season, and as time went on she had thought that they had made their minds up not to have any more children and Vicky couldn't help but think that maybe this was a sensible decision for them to have made, as Lindsay appeared to have suffered with severe depression after the birth of Callum. Vicky hoped she said all the right things—"Congratulations--that's wonderful news---It will be good for Callum to have a sister or brother, I'm so happy for you both."

Bruce drove her into town so that she could do some present shopping for Jane's two boys. She found it difficult to concentrate. She bought a book on Scottish Castles for Henry and a tie and ceremonial dirk for William, a congratulations card to give to Lindsay and Bruce. Vicky asked him in the car as they drove back if he would tell Lindsay that she knew she was pregnant,-

"I don't want to put my foot in it if she wanted to wait before she told me."

"Yes, of course I will tell her, only we haven't told Callum yet, so perhaps we ought to do that first. We will leave it for Lindsay to tell you herself. That will be best." he said.

That evening, after Callum had enjoyed another lesson on Tweed and was now safely tucked up in bed, she broached the subject with Lindsay of her buying Tweed for him. "He's got such a wonderfully steady temperament and I think Callum would love him. What do you think?" Vicky pleaded." May I?"

"He's never been interested before Vicky. I wouldn't bother if I were you, besides I haven't the time to teach him now, and I've little enough grass as it is for Jet without having a greedy Highland pony."

"Oh", once again Vicky felt snubbed and then she thought, maybe it's because she is pregnant and doesn't want anymore workload. This, she could understand. But why didn't she tell her?

The next morning Vicky had a bad conscience over the ironing which had now overflowed into three baskets. Poor Lindsay, she must be feeling the strain of her pregnancy, she would do her a good turn but as she put the ironing board up in the kitchen, Lindsay started to take her own clothes out of the baskets saying that she liked to do her own trousers and tops and underwear herself.

Vicky couldn't help thinking that it was alright for her to iron Callum's and Bruce's clothes but obviously her ironing would not do for her. Once again she felt that Lindsay had snubbed her. As she ironed, dark thoughts filled her mind until she became quite depressed. It was as though Lindsay was not pleased to see her. As it was she and Bruce had done the shopping, cooked the meals, washed up and done the housework. Lindsay had spent little time with them. She hadn't even acknowledged or sympathised with her over the loss of her husband Ian, not once.

Vicky aired the clothes and then folded them into neat piles to be put away leaving the one basket of Lindsay's clothes for her to do. She felt that she would have to have a breath of fresh air and clear her head of all the uncomfortable resentments she was feeling. She would go for a ride on

Tweed. Although Bruce had warned her that he thought the woodland she had ridden through when she saw the birds of prey, could be private, she chose to ignore it and found herself turning Tweed into the wood. They followed one of its many twisting paths. A soothing balm fell upon Vicky dispelling her former mood. It was a deciduous woodland with a variety of birch, hazel, beech and oak with only the odd pine or larch. It was spring. There were bluebells, archangel, stitchwort and celandine to delight the eye. She started to hum softly to herself. They turned a corner of the path and were startled to come face to face with a young woman standing quietly before them. In her surprise Vicky dropped her riding crop, for the scene that stood before her looked like something from a medieval painting.

The girl appeared to be dressed in a dark green doublet and hose, although on later reflection she was probably wearing green velvet-cord jodhpurs and a leather waistcoat over a green jersey. Her long golden hair, worn loose but tightly waved in the style made famous by the Pre-Raphaelites, tumbled around her face and over her shoulders upon which a very large golden plumed bird of prey sat perched with huge talons, fixing them with a gimlet stare. Tweed, perhaps feeling the tension blew down his nose, shook his bridle noisily and tried to turn around.

"Stay where you are." the girl ordered them peremptorily as the bird suddenly rose up, in all its magnificence, stretching its huge wings out as though to enfold the girl from any danger or to attack them.

"He's just very protective of me," she explained. "I will get your crop," the girl crooned in a soothing way as she stooped down very slowly on one knee to retrieve it, the bird balancing still with outstretched wings on her shoulder. She held the crop out for Vicky to take. The sun shone from behind her, glinting through the leaves of the trees and catching her golden hair and bronzing every subtle shade of feather in the magnificent bird's outstretched wings. Vicky wished in that instant that she could have captured this picture of them on camera. She could see that the girl wore a falconer's tough leather glove and was loosely tied to her hand. And, as she turned her head to look at the bird, she revealed a somewhat aquiline hawkish nose, like the bird on her shoulder. She stroked him on his breast and slowly he folded his wings. She smiled and said simply, "He loves me."

"Is it an eagle?" Vicky asked?

"Yes, it's a golden eagle."

"He's beautiful." The girl fixed piercing ice-blue eyes on Vicky and asked,

"Where were you going?"

"Oh, I was just having a ride through this wood." Vicky answered. The girl smiled faintly, "Where have you come from?"

"From 'the Croft,'--- up this glen. I'm visiting my son. I'm Vicky Lewis."

"Oh,--- you're Bruce's mother?"

"Yes, do you know him and Lindsay?" The girl smiled as though the question amused her but didn't answer her.

"I'm Fiona," she offered, "I live up at the house here with my father. These are our woods. They are private and you are trespassing," she said cooly.

"Oh,----- I'm very sorry." Vicky said, feeling like a naughty schoolgirl. She was taken aback by this forthright girl more or less telling her off. She felt her face reddening before the stare of this haughty young woman. Who did she think she was? What a cheek! She backed Tweed away from her, before turning him round. As she walked away she felt the eyes of the girl, Fiona, and the gimlet eyes of the eagle on her back as they trotted off. Back at The Croft she related her adventure to Bruce.

"She seemed to know who you were." Bruce shook his head,

"No, I don't know her, but if it's the same place where this man keeps birds of prey, I would very much like to meet him,------- or his daughter. She sounds intriguing," he laughed, "if not a little frightening !"

*   *   *

They all drove with her to the airport. Callum was sorry to see her go. Last night his mum had told him that Tweed would have to go back to the Gilchrists and it had nearly made him cry. Vicky felt powerless to interfere in the decision. They had had fun together and she would not leave it so long before she saw him again. Lindsay was charming to her now that she was going, insisting that she came to see her off. Bruce had sat on her bed with her that morning when he brought her a cup of tea.

"Look, mum, I know this is a difficult time for you, selling up and looking for somewhere smaller. Lindsay and I had a chat last night about you living with us in the housekeeper's flat. We would love to have you mum. I know you have always said that you would never live with either Jane or myself but I want you to think about living here with us, or, if you want to be more independent and take a cottage nearby, we can help you do that." Vicky was touched by their concern. She felt that it was a little incredulous that Lindsay had really wanted her to live with them. Nevertheless she thanked him and told him she would consider it.

With kisses and hugs and a newspaper to read on the journey back, they waved her off.

*   *   *

"Guess who I saw the other day," Fiona said archly to her father as she placed a bowl of soup before him.

"How on earth, should I know?" She sat down and kept him waiting as she placed a napkin across her knees and lifted a spoonful of soup to her lips.

"Your lady-friend, the one you told me about,---- the one you met by the loch.---Victoria, no less."

"Now, how do you know it was her?"

"She was on her way to see you, riding through our wood on a Highland pony,---- just like the Queen." she teased.

"Good God ! Well, I didn't see her."

"No, I told her she was trespassing, and sent her packing."

"You did what?" he roared. "You shouldn't have done that, how very discourteous of you Fiona," he was suddenly angry and surprised by his feeling of disappointment that he hadn't seen her. She had made him laugh again and she had told him that she too was sad with her loss as he was with his and somehow sharing their loss, it had felt good. He had looked forward to seeing her again. A tangible silence grew between them. Fiona knew that she had been right. Her father's reaction confirmed the feeling she had when he had first related meeting this woman. She could tell that the woman had made an impression upon him and although she felt sorry for his loneliness she didn't want anyone else to take her own mother's place in his life. After all, he had her.

"Well, I shall certainly never see her again," he muttered.

"It's not important, is it?" Fiona asked sharply.

"She was just a very nice woman,------ and yes, I would have liked to have seen her again." Fiona shrugged, unrepentant, "I was just protecting our estate against trespass father." She got up from her chair and went and put her arms around him, "You've always got me daddy." He smiled, "I know I have, my darling."

*   *   *

Vicky sat back in her seat on the plane and reviewed her thoughts over the past week. Lindsay had been utterly charming and attentive with her this morning but still nothing had been said about her being pregnant and so Vicky had not revealed to her that Bruce had told her and she had not congratulated her or given her the card she had bought. Something was not right, perhaps she didn't want the child? Should she tell Jane, her daughter? but first she was going back to Wales to see the estate agent, and solicitor, sign the contract and arrange to put her things in storage while she thought where she wanted to live, either near Bruce or near Jane. Her week away had not restored or comforted her, the only time she had laughed was with her grandson Callum, and that strange encounter in the mountains with John Brown where they had shared and laughed together. The rest had been anxiety. She thought about the ring that she and Bruce had found. Guiltily she had not mentioned it to Lindsay. She fished it out of her pocket and slipped it on her finger and admired it. It was very beautiful. When she visited Jane in London she would make enquiries about it, as to its provenance.

*   *   *

PART TWO

1865

The Queen was lonely after her husband's death. She had looked to him for everything. Her two daughters, Vicky and Alice were both married and couldn't fulfil the companionship that their mother longed for as they both lived in Germany and visiting mother had become inconvenient for them. Both daughters noticed that the only occasions on which their mother appeared content were when John Brown was attending to her needs at Balmoral. It was therefore arranged that the ghillie John Brown should be in permanent attendance on the Queen. The plan worked and there were less frequent demands on the family. Mr. Brown became Her Majesty's personal servant.

*   *   *

CHAPTER FOUR

After Vicky had signed the contract and handed the keys of the farmhouse to the solicitor she sat in her car and felt emotionless. A part of her life was now over. She would not go back and take one long last look at the farmhouse with its beautiful but difficult hill-farming land where it was only possible to keep sheep. Her life here had ended with Ian's death. It was no longer hers. For better or for worse she had severed the long ties there. A blank page lay before her. A new life, living closer to her daughter Jane, in London. Perhaps a little flat? Or a cottage near Bruce, her son, in Scotland? She suddenly shook herself. She would not speculate about her future, it made her feel hemmed in and panicky. She buckled the seat belt across herself, flipped her mobile open and told Jane she was on her way. She drove the same route that she and her husband had taken whenever they visited Jane, through the Cotswolds, by-passing Oxford where she stopped for lunch at a small familiar village inn. Vicky found dining on her own in a pub a real trial. Food stuck in her throat as people glanced at her with curiosity seated alone at a table. She had taken to reading a book or the newspaper which had made her feel less conspicuous, It was as though she wore the word widow on her forehead. Sometimes she and her husband had stayed the night there to break the journey but Vicky was glad to be on her way again, continuing cross-country through Bicester, Aylesbury, Hemel Hempstead and then just a little way on the M25, and off through Epping Forest to Woodford Green. If you had to live close to London for business it was a pleasant place to live. People still referred to it as, the village.

Jane and her husband Mark and their two boys, Henry and William, lived in a pleasant tree-lined road of family Victorian villas. It was term- time and the boys were away at their boarding school.

As Vicky parked her car on their drive, Jane opened the door and flung her arms around her mother and kissed her. Mark, her chartered surveyor husband, stood behind smiling. He was a tall fair-haired fresh-faced, typical good-looking Englishman who played cricket and golf. He towered above his wife as he greeted Vicky and took her bags. Jane was petite, her dark hair drawn back into a chignon, large expressive eyes, looking every inch the ballet dancer she had been, but since her marriage and motherhood, she now taught, passing on her gift to a younger generation of would-be dancers.

After Vicky had freshened up and changed into a dress and they were all having a pre-dinner drink in the sitting room, Jane questioned her mother's trip to Scotland. As Vicky recounted her bewilderment over her daughter-in-law's behaviour she tried hard to be fair to Lindsay, saying, that perhaps they were expecting Lindsay to conform to their ways whereas she had been brought up in a different way.

"I just wish I could believe that, mum." Jane said, "but I can't." There was no love lost between Jane and her brother's wife, Lindsay. She had been disappointed that her brother had married such a seemingly ungracious girl, who was always moaning about her brother with whom she had had a close relationship. They too had stopped visiting after the time they had driven up there with Henry and William when they were much younger. It had been a long journey which lasted nearly eleven hours and had exhausted them and their ingenuity in keeping the boys from boredom, only to find that when they arrived, Lindsay and Bruce were nowhere to be found. Lindsay eventually appeared from the potting shed and asked them to put the kettle on and amuse themselves. The rest of their so-called holiday was spent in stocking the fridge and planning meals with Bruce. They had vowed that they would never be tempted again to visit her brother which was a shame for Callum, an only child, who would never really get to know his cousins.

"How did you find Callum?" Jane asked.

"Oh, he really is a lovely boy, a bit neglected and left to his own devices, but he is a happy undemanding child. I loved him to bits."

"And Bruce?" Her mother shrugged and pulled a face. "Living in the usual chaos, trying to hold everything together, I think. He loves her. He told me that he thought she was a lovely girl."

"Mm?" Jane murmured wryly.

Mark listened but diplomatically kept silent. He saw Lindsay in a slightly different light. On the few occasions when he had met her she had embarrassed him by laying on the charm and flirting with him when she was in his company and ignoring Bruce. It had not escaped Jane's notice either.

"Bruce told me that they were having another baby, but Lindsay never said anything to me and it was strange, because I felt that I couldn't say anything either. It all felt very awkward. If you ring Bruce, don't say anything, will you, unless they mention it to you."

"No, of course not, but how strange. Perhaps she doesn't want another child?"

"They offered me a home with them."

"Did they?" Jane and Mark exchanged looks at this piece of news.

"We want you to come and live near us," Jane said firmly, "Mark has found lots of flats and apartments for us to go and see in the next few days. There is so much for you to do here mum. Remember how we loved going to London together. You would be bored stiff out in the wilds with those two. We are really looking forward to you living here." she said firmly. *But not with you.* Vicky couldn't help thinking even though she had no intention of living with either of her children. It never worked out, but at least Bruce and Lindsay had offered

*   *   *

They were in the cafe at Harrods. "I'll get the coffee, mum. You grab a table," Jane said. Vicky was grateful to sit down after an exhausting morning looking at flats and apartments, all at phenomenal prices, she thought. It was so depressing. Had she been a fool to sell the farmhouse and land together? She could have managed with just the house. She looked for Jane standing at the back of a slow moving queue, and then turned quickly as she heard a man's voice say, "Ma'am, your servant." and looked up with amazement into the face of John Brown. They both started to say,

"What are you doing------ here?" And broke off with a laugh. He took the seat beside her. Jane, noticed these proceedings from the queue and watched with a puzzled frown on her face as the man beckoned a young woman seated at another table to join him and her mother. The young woman, dressed in a rather avant-garde way in a dark green velvet cloak and with a mass of blonde tresses tumbling around her face, got up and joined them. She watched as the girl sat back in her chair without greeting her mother, except for a little nod of her golden head.

The man and her mother were in deep conversation as Jane came with a tray of coffee. Vicky introduced her to Mr. John Brown and his daughter, Fiona, friends she had met when she was in Scotland. Jane noticed that her mother's tired, jaded look had been visibly replaced by a much younger looking woman who blushed and laughed and talked effusively like a teen-ager whilst she and his daughter Fiona, sat back without speaking and cooly observed their respective parent's behaviour.

"But what are you doing here?" Vicky wanted to know.

"I'm escorting my daughter back to her University," he said with a smile at Fiona, "and fulfilling an engagement at the Natural History Museum here. Killing two birds with one stone, you might say. And what are you doing here, might I ask, ma'am.?"

"Well, Brown." Vicky said adopting an imperious tone of voice, "I'm looking for another royal residence, with my daughter's help." smiling at Jane.

Jane looked at Fiona who met her startled look and rolled her ice-blue eyes heavenward as much as to say, *Ye Gods!*

"How can you think of living in London?" he said suddenly seriously concerned, and then remembering himself. "That was rude of me, please forgive me. It's none of my business." Vicky waved his apology aside, with "It's my official place Brown, ----and there's always Balmoral to escape to," she added mischievously. John smiled, hugely enjoying the royal banter.

Fiona coughed, "I really think that we had better be going, father" and she stood up. He slipped a card in front of Vicky, "Please ring me whilst you are in London and we can meet up again if you like?" To Jane's amazement, she heard her mother say,

"Yes, I would like that." They all shook hands before he and Fiona departed. Jane put her glasses on the end of her nose and surveyed her mother quizzically,

"Well, what was all that about?"

"What?"

"All that, Ma'am, royal residences, Balmoral, and calling him Brown."

"It's just our joke, I'm Victoria, he is John Brown. Can you believe it?" she said smiling delightedly at her daughter.

"No, I can't." Jane said drily.

*　　*　　*

Later that evening after her mother had gone to bed, Jane, passing her mother's room heard her talking to someone. She couldn't help pausing to listen. Her mother sounded animated as she laughed and appeared to be arranging a time to see someone. She thought she could guess who. She made her way downstairs to tell Mark about the strange meeting this morning with two strangers over coffee and now, perhaps her mother was arranging another meeting.

"What do you think we should do about it?" she asked Mark. Mark was watching television. He looked up at Jane with a look of amusement on his face.

"Why should we do anything?"

"Mother doesn't know anything about him or his daughter. Why should he suddenly turn up out of the blue this morning after she had just met him in Scotland last week. It's too much of a coincidence. Men can prey on lonely women, like my mother, you know. You should have seen her positively flirting with him. Do you think I should ring Bruce? See if he knows who he is?"

"Well, if you like." Mark said doubtfully. "Personally, I think that you shouldn't interfere. I'm amazed that you have been eavesdropping on her." Jane had the grace to blush. Nevertheless, after glancing at her watch, although it was late, she left the room to phone Bruce in privacy. She heard the phone ringing and prayed that Lindsay wouldn't answer it. For one thing she could never get a word in edgeways. Lindsay would talk endlessly and boringly, never interested in what anyone else had to say, until she felt like screaming. She was relieved when Bruce's deep voice said,

"Hello?-- Jane?" He sounded surprised, "Is mum alright?" He listened, then, "I don't know the man or his daughter. I know that she met them and that they live up the glen. He has something to do with the Wildlife Trust here, I think. There's nothing to worry about. Mum can look after herself." Jane sniffed, "You haven't seen them together, mother is ---is embarrassing to say the least." Bruce laughed,

"She's feeling the loneliness, without dad, that's all."

"Older women can be stupid, and she is very vulnerable. Men can prey on widows."

"What? You think he's after her money?" Bruce chortled. He couldn't wait to tell Lindsay.

"Look here", he said, "We ought to feel grateful that mum has found a friend. It absolves us from worrying about her, feeling that we have got to make up for dad, if you know what I mean. It's better than her being unhappy surely?"

"Well, we'll see." Jane said tight lipped.

*   *   *

CHAPTER FIVE

Over breakfast, Jane said, "I have to take some classes this morning. Would you like to come and watch, mother, and then perhaps we can get a bite of lunch and go and have a look at some more apartments?"

"I would have enjoyed watching the classes, but maybe another time dear, because I've arranged to meet the gentleman we met yesterday, Mr. Brown."

"Oh? Is that wise mother. You barely know him. This isn't the country. This is London. What are you going to do for heaven sakes?" She asked curiously. Vicky laughed a little self-consciously, "Well, I'm going to take a taxi to the Victoria and Albert Museum and see what they can tell me about the ring that Bruce found in the loch, and then afterwards, Mr Brown is taking me to lunch."

"So, you've told him all about this ring?"

"Sort of. Why not? Why the third degree Jane? You are making me feel like a child." Jane sighed resignedly, looked at her watch, "Okay mum, I'm sorry. I've got to fly now, see you later---- and take care." She wanted to add, and don't be so trusting, but thought better of it!

Vicky took a taxi to the Victoria and Albert, climbed the steps and approached an official as to where she should go to have her ring looked at by an expert in Victorian jewellery. "I'm sorry Madam," he said, "Yes, it's true that people can bring items in to be assessed here, but it is every other Tuesday and this is the wrong Tuesday.---- If you could come back next Tuesday madam?" he added hopefully. "Or photograph it and send the photo with a letter."

"Oh," Vicky said disappointed. "Thank you anyway." She didn't quite know now what to do with herself before she had arranged to meet John Brown. In the end she decided to go and have a look at the jewellery in the museum and see if she could see anything as distinctive as her ring. As she browsed around the glass covered cases there were many beautiful Victorian rings but none quite like hers and she felt sure, with a tingle down her spine, that it really must be a royal ring. She looked up as she felt someone's close presence beside her.

"Hello, I thought I might find you here," he said. "Any luck?" John Brown's face smiled down at her with his clear blue eyes, so like his daughter's, but with a warmth about them as he looked at her. Vicky thought.

"No, Can you believe it? It was the wrong day."

"Oh dear, never mind. You can always come again. Let me take you to lunch" he said, taking her arm as they walked out into the spring sunshine.

"London looks so beautiful when the weather is like this." Vicky said to him. "All this beautiful architecture and magnificent statues. It is a very grand and special place. I know I'm a country girl at heart, but there has always been something about London for me."

"Well,- yes." he concurred. A little unwillingly, she thought.

"It's not Scotland," he said, smiling down at her. "I suppose I have the best of both worlds, I quite often come here on business."

He took her to an Italian bistro. The counter top was laden with bowls and trays of colourful authentic mediterranean dishes, sardines, tomatoes, olives, jewelled baked peppers, and pastas. The place was crowded with business people but he had reserved a table for them. They sat down and he ordered two glasses of red wine with their meal.

"I hope I've got it right. I took a chance that you would like the food. I tend to always come here when I'm in this part of London."

"I love it." Vicky said. "To tell you the truth, this is much better than looking at apartments, which I was supposed to be doing with my daughter this morning." and she raised her glass.

"Oh dear, I hope I haven't got you into any trouble."

"The trouble with children is, that when you reach a certain age they think that they have got to parent you," she said.

"Yes, I know what you mean. Since Catriona died, Fiona has taken it upon herself to be like a guard-dog." They both laughed.

"I know this isn't my business but are you serious about living in London?" She sighed, "I've burnt my boats I'm afraid—sold the farm---I loved it, but it was in a very remote position. The land was difficult for me to manage on my own and when my husband died the children thought that it was not practical for me to stay there----and I was lonely after my husband died," she added.

"I suppose I didn't take the advice that every body tells you to do, to wait for a year or two and then see how you feel, before you think of moving." Her eyes filled with tears,----" but life, I believe, falls into chapters, and this is just going to be a different chapter." She shrugged her shoulders and smiled bravely.

"I shall have the pleasure of seeing my son and daughter more often and my grandchildren. In fact we are all going to an open day at their school this weekend. I'm looking forward to that."

"Now, what about you?" she asked.

"What do you mean?"

"Well, you say that you often come to London?" He smiled, "Yes, I come several times a year, actually. I brought Fiona down for her new term at University. She's in her last year now. I stay at my club and see old colleagues. And sometimes I give a paper at the Natural History Museum here and bring along some stuffed birds or mammals with me for their collection." She pulled a face. He raised his hands, palm upwards and shrugged, "It's the nature of my work back home in Scotland. Now, tell me about this ring. Is that it?" he asked catching hold of her hand. "I've kept on noticing it. It is very beautiful." She took it off and handed it to him. As he studied the ring she told him how Bruce had found it lying on a shale shelf of the loch at the waters edge, after she had got back into the boat the morning they had met. And then she thought how extraordinary it was that she had met this John Brown again, in London of all places.

"It's certainly worth trying to get an expert on its provenance." he said, handing it back to her. "You could try Sotheby's Jewellery department, New Bond Street." He looked at his watch, "It's not too late. I'll come with you, if you like. We can get a taxi there."

Vicky went to the Ladies Room first in order to phone Jane and tell her that she might be a little later than expected. She was relieved when Jane appeared to be out and the answer phone switched on. She left a brief message for her before taking a taxi to Sotheby's.

Once inside, they went up to the desk to be directed where to go. John said that he wouldn't go up in the lift with her but browse around the art that was hung for inspection prior to auction. Vicky went up to the next floor in a tiny chintzy lift and felt foolish when the lift stopped but the door didn't open and then discovered that a door had opened behind her which led into a room where a stylishly dressed young woman sitting behind a desk looked up as Vicky emerged from the lift. She took her name and then asked her to wait, indicating for her to take a seat. Another woman was sitting on a plush leather settee waiting. She was undoing a rolled up leather travel bag which held jewellery. The young woman behind the desk beckoned the woman over and she started to lay out diamond rings, pearl necklaces, and earrings, gold brooches with beautiful stones of emerald and sapphire before the young woman for her appraisal.

Vicky speculated whether she was having to sell because she had fallen on hard times, or was getting a divorce perhaps? She did look sad, she thought. But maybe it was merely an insurance evaluation. She was shocked that there was no privacy for the transaction. Vicky thought how easy it would be for a jewel-thief to travel up on the one-man tiny lift, jam it, snatch up the jewels and depart the way he came. She gave herself a little shake. She really must control her imagination. Forms were being signed. The woman got up and left and the jewellery was put in a box and taken out.

When the young woman returned, she beckoned Vicky to come to the desk. "I'm so sorry to have kept you waiting, Mrs Lewis." She smiled charmingly at her and extended her hand, "I'm Madison Haynes, How can I help you? Is it an evaluation or do you want us to sell at auction?"

"Well, no, neither really, at the moment. You see my son found this ring in a loch near the Balmoral estate and because it bears a crown with an A underneath, we wondered whether it could have anything to do with Queen Victoria and Prince Albert,----- maybe a mourning ring? We know that Victoria visited the loch with Prince Albert and also with John Brown."

Madison Haynes studied the ring, "It is beautifully made," she murmured, "It is certainly Victorian but I am not sure that it is an Imperial crown. Just one moment," she said, and disappeared through a door behind her desk. She came back a little later. "In view of where the ring was discovered and the detail on the intaglio, our initial impression is that the ring could have direct provenance to Queen Victoria and His Royal Highness Prince Albert. This is most exciting." She smiled broadly at Vicky, obviously excited at the thought. "However, our European Heraldry Consultant, is not here at the moment and we would like you to leave the ring with us so that he can confirm its provenance."

"How long for?" Vicky asked.

"It could be two weeks. I will take your phone number and address." Vicky, in a daze descended in the lift clutching a receipt for the ring. John was waiting for her, "Well?" He asked.

"They seem to think that it really might be Queen Victoria's ring !" she said with suppressed excitement.

"Oh, my word ! To think that the ring, a part of Scotland's history could end up being sold to the highest bidder in a London auction room and might end up in America, or Japan---or goodness knows where. It's rather sad, don't you think?"

"But I have no intention of selling it." she protested. "I only wanted to know what they thought about it. Besides, it really belongs to Bruce, he found it. I'm just keeping it for him. It will always stay in Scotland, I promise." He smiled down at her. "Good. Come on, let's go and find a cup of tea."

Over a cup of tea he told her that he would be returning to Scotland at the weekend. "I've enjoyed today immensely and I do hope Vicky that you will let me know what happens about the ring and that we may meet again, if not here— perhaps in Scotland?"

"Yes, of course." she said lightly, but thought that they were two lonely people, grasping at this unusual friendship which, because of distance would in all probability not be maintained. She felt sad and fell silent. He persisted, "You have my mobile phone number?" She nodded.

"And I've got yours. So, we'll keep in touch?" John accompanied her in a taxi back to his club in Knightsbridge and instructed the driver to take Vicky back to Jane's address. He kissed her lightly on the cheek, "Goodbye dear Vicky." She felt his lips brush her cheek. As he had bent over her she had a ridiculous impulse to touch the curls of hair clustered thickly around the nape of his neck. Of course she didn't. Whatever would he have thought of her if she had? He waved her off. Driving back she reviewed the day. They had only met three times. Twice very briefly yet there had been no awkwardness. It was if they had known each other for years.

As Vicky walked up the drive after alighting from the taxi she glanced at her watch. Jane must have been looking out for her, for the front door opened and she stood in the doorway waiting. She must be late and had caused concern, she thought guiltily.

"Mother, where on earth have you been. I've been so worried."

"I left you a message on the answer-phone to tell you I would be a little late. Did you try the answer phone?" Vicky

49

said with some asperity in her voice. She had had a lovely time with John and had been feeling calm and happy. Now, she was feeling decidedly put out by her daughter's attitude.

"Oh, no. I'm sorry mother. I was just a little concerned for you. Come in and tell me all about your day. I'll put the kettle on." Jane said trying to make amends. Vicky put her hand up. "No thank you dear, I've had tea. I just need to sit down. Walking the pavements of London has tired me out." As Vicky had raised her hand, Jane's quick eyes had noticed that her mother was no longer wearing the ring and couldn't help thinking that maybe it lay in John Brown's pocket. It was a disgraceful thought for her to have. She couldn't ever remember being like this—as though her very mind was being poisoned by the man himself. They sat down in two comfy armchairs.

"How did you get on at the Victoria and Albert?" she asked her mother. Vicky laughed, "Went on the wrong day, didn't I? but never mind, John took me to a very nice place for lunch."

"Where's the ring then? You haven't left it with this man, have you?"

"I was going to tell you all about it, Jane, but I don't like your attitude." Vicky got to her feet. "I'm going to my room. Please don't disturb me." and made a dignified exit trying to conceal the tumult of indignation and hurt that her daughter could vilify her friendship with John Brown. It was obvious that Jane didn't like him, was suspicious of him. She didn't like being put in the position of defending him. It was outrageous.

Jane and Mark dined alone. "I'm not surprised she's taken offence." Mark said, after Jane had recounted the conversation with her mother. "Poor chap, you've really got it in for him, haven't you?"

"I'm just trying to protect her, that's all. She's probably given him this ring."

"So, what if she has? --- it's not ours, is it? She has a right to do whatever she wants to do with the damn ring."

"I cannot believe that my father has only been dead just over a year and my mother is already flirting with another man."

"Now steady on Jane," Mark cautioned.

CHAPTER SIX

As Vicky sat watching Jane teach a class, she remembered when she had taken her as a very small child to ballet classes. Living on a farm and lacking the company of other children to play with, Vicky thought that ballet classes with other little children would solve the problem and take away her loneliness and shyness. Vicky certainly had never imagined that her shy little girl would be an outstanding pupil from the start, winning a scholarship at the age of ten with The Royal Academy and then a place at the upper school of the Royal Ballet, finally taking her place with the Company and that she would be dividing her time between the farm and London. Looking back, she seemed to have spent years sitting in a small octagonal waiting room, listening to piano music, Chopin, Tchaikovsky, Liszt, drifting down the stairs from the studio above, enveloping her in its beauty while she waited for her daughter to finish classes. Familiar snatches came unbidden into her mind at odd moments down through the years. It had been years of gruelling training for the comparatively short life of the dancer. To Jane it had been the fulfilment of her dreams. Now, she enjoyed passing on the vision and the dream to her pupils. Vicky loved to watch her taking the class, until one particular girl would draw her eye to her again and again. A sense of presence, an indefinable something else, that showed a natural gift, a promise. It was always fascinating and exciting to her. From the barre work, the plies, grandes- battements, port de bras, where Jane's eagle eye corrected and encouraged and demonstrated, to the centre practice, the fouettes, pirouettes, adage, allegro and a dance study with pointe work until finally, the reverence, a deep curtsy from pupil to teacher at the end. Throughout it all, Vicky sat spellbound.

Afterwards, over lunch she liked discussing with Jane which pupils had impressed her. It had been a very satisfactory morning, she thought. Jane brought out another list of flats and apartments for them to see and was studying a map to plan where to start. It filled Vicky with a strange sense of reluctance, but she supposed she had better show willing. She had to find somewhere to live, but so far nothing appealed and they all seemed far beyond her means. It all seemed so drastically different from the farmhouse in the wilds. Somehow she must come to terms with the fact that it was going to be different. She put on what she hoped was an optimistic face.

As they were finishing their coffee, Jane turned to her mother with a confidential air,

"You know mother, Mark and I have been considering moving closer into London, it would make things so much easier for me to get to the studios. Mark has found something that might suit all of us, it incorporates a self-contained flat." She looked into her mother's face with questioning raised eye-brows. "What do you think? Shall we go and see it?"

"Alright dear." Vicky said in a non-committal way, but feeling that in some way a noose was tightening, that there was an inevitability about it and somehow she was in danger of losing all autonomy over her affairs with this new idea of Jane and Mark's. Vicky asked to see the agents papers on the property. It was in an attractive part of Kensington with the Gardens opposite. She turned to the last page and gasped when she saw the price,

"My God, Jane! I don't have this sort of money."

"Let's see it first and then we can discuss it with Mark tonight. After all it's only the first one we've looked at where we share." Jane persuaded.

As they walked around the apartment with the agent extolling its virtues, Vicky was not impressed. The self-contained flat was within a nice spacious apartment she conceded, but the flat itself was very small indeed and she felt that it would soon become like a prison to her. Fine for Jane and Mark, but what about her? There was Kensington Gardens which was very beautiful now with its trees sporting their vibrant new green leaves fluttering in the spring breeze. That would be a plus, to walk beside the water of the Serpentine. and maybe she could have a dog. Could I be happy here, she asked herself?

"I think it has lots of advantages for the children and you would be here for them, mother, in the holidays." Jane said positively.

That evening, around the dinner table the financing of such a project was discussed. Vicky remained rather unco-operative in not revealing how much capital she had, not because she didn't trust them both, she did, but over the years she had learned that situations can change rapidly with divorce, with illness, with death, and wondered where exactly she might be placed in such a situation, God forbid it might ever happen but she heard alarm bells.

Miserably, she wondered what Ian, her late husband, would have her do? But as ever there was only a terrible empty silence. She longed for a friend who could give her a dispassionate appraisal of her options. She felt tempted to ring John Brown and see what he thought. Everyone else, she felt, had a vested interest. A few hours elapsed. She looked at her watch. Was it too late to ring him up now? She dialled his mobile number. When she heard his voice she apologised for the late hour. Should she call him back tomorrow? He smiled at her rush of words and anxiety. "No, not at all. It is really nice to hear from you." She told him about viewing the flat within the apartment. How nice that it was so close to Kensington Gardens, even though it would be a bit poky for her-------" there was a silence------ she was waiting for him to say something.

"Do I sense that you have a gut feeling of panic about this?" he asked putting his finger on her anxiety.

"Yes, I suppose I do, I feel that I am being rushed into a decision that I may regret, but that everybody else is relying upon. Oh, it's so difficult. I don't know what to do. I feel that I am wasting their time as well as my own."

"Well Vicky, it is always wise to listen to your inner voice, your gut feeling. After your bereavement you need time to adjust You shouldn't be making life-changing decisions for at least a couple of years.."

"But I've already done that by selling the farm in Wales. I can't put the clock back. I felt, at the time, that it was the right thing to do, but now---"

"Okay. It may well have been the right decision. All I'm saying, is that you don't have to fit in with anyone else's plans if you are not a hundred per cent sure that it is right for you."

"The trouble is, that inflation is pushing property prices up and if I don't make a decision soon, I may not have enough money.--- I just needed to run all this past someone who is independent but a friend. Thank you for listening John," she said.

"Look Vicky, thank you for confiding in me. I'm honoured that you did. Don't rush into anything yet. If you haven't got inner harmony something is telling you that it is wrong, okay?"

"Okay, I'm sure you are right, thank you again John, Goodnight."

*　　*　　*

The day was warm and sunny as Mark drove them to the boys open day. Old scented Lime trees lined the drive up to Stanage School. It was an imposing edifice surrounded on all sides with lawned grounds. They drove to the parking area and walked back to where a cricket match was in progress. Henry, the younger boy, had been looking out for them. He ran up to them looking smart in his white flannels, shirt and pullover. It was not his time to bat yet. He was a serious, earnest boy of ten with a mop of unruly hair. He shook hands with his father and kissed his mother and grandmother Vicky. Once they were seated, he pointed out to them where William was fielding out in mid-field. After the match William came over, breathless and with fine beads of sweat on his handsome tanned face, two years older than Henry, yet there was no mistaking that they were brothers. Both boys spoke well and had impeccable manners. Vicky had brought their presents with her from Scotland. Henry rather wished that she had bought the dirk for him instead of for William and handled it longingly, before reluctantly giving it back to William, but he was much too good mannered to appear ungrateful for his book on Castles. "When you are older, I'll buy you a dirk too," she promised.

Vicky couldn't help but compare their lives with their cousin Callum. Jane and her husband Mark, were giving their boys every advantage of a good private education whereas Callum had a somewhat neglectful home life without plans for any special schooling. This, she thought, looking around her, was like a greenhouse for the growth of special plants, compared to the rough and tumble of a wild plants survival. Which would turn out to be the best, she wondered.

Later, there was a strawberry and cream tea. A look at some of the boys work, and a word with their various Masters, followed by prize- giving in the grand medieval hall. Afterwards, they rounded off the day by taking the boys out for dinner at a local hotel. It had been a highlight day for all of them. They dropped the boys back at school and Henry clung a little to his mother as the final goodbyes were said. He had been here since he was eight and for all their advantages he must miss a normal home life and Vicky's heart went out to him. Maybe it was better to be a wild plant, after all, she thought.

*   *   *

CHAPTER SEVEN

The next morning at breakfast Vicky had a letter. It was from Sotheby's

Dear Mrs Lewis,

I am writing with regards to the gold and bloodstone intaglio ring that you brought in for appraisal to Sotheby's on the 5th June 2009. In the light of the geographical location where it was discovered and the apparent detail on the intaglio, our initial impression was that the ring might have a direct provenance to Queen Victoria and HRH Prince Albert.

However, after a more detailed examination by our European Heraldry Consutant, we can confirm that the crest is of baronial provenance. We would thus value the ring to have an auction estimate of £2,000. I do hope that this news does not come as too much of a disappointment to you as I fully appreciate what an excitement it would have been had the ring been linked directly to HRH Prince Albert! Please let me know if you would like to enter it into sale, so that I can prepare the correct paper work, or whether you would like to come and collect the ring in due course.

Many kind regards, Yours sincerely,
Madison Haynes.
Sotheby's Jewellery Department, London.

Vicky felt a twinge of disappointment. She wondered what European House the crest did represent and whether it was possible to know. They hadn't said. After all, HRH Prince Albert was of the House of Saxe – Coburg and Gotha, Germany. Queen Victoria's daughters, Alice and Vicky had married into a similar European House; might not that be the connection? She certainly wasn't going to let it go for auction. She would ring them and go and collect it.

Jane could hardly conceal her curiosity. Who would be writing to her mother at her address, she wondered. Vicky passed the letter over to her daughter for her to see. Jane was embarrassed that she had accused her mother of having given the ring to John Brown, when all the time it had been at Sotheby's.

"Oh it's no big deal then, the ring," she said dismissing it. And then a moment later, "I'm sorry mother, I thought you had given it away, ----Forgive me for saying what I did? Vicky smiled and nodded.

"I should put it up for auction, if I were you."

"No, I don't think so. For one thing, it's not mine. Bruce found it"

"But he gave it to you."

"Yes, I know, but it is rightfully his and it will go to him when I die." Jane looked at her mother but made no comment. She took a deep breath before asking, "Going back to the apartment in Kensington, have you thought anymore about it mother?"

"No, not really."

"Only,--- we don't want to lose it. We want to put in an offer before someone else does."

"The flat is very small and more to the point Jane, I can't afford it."

"Oh, but we would help you mother."

"I want to be independent and I feel that it is just not right for me----I'm really sorry, dear." she said as Jane's face fell.

Vicky felt Jane's disappointment over what she had said. It had been an awkward conversation yet she suddenly felt a great relief that she had done what John had advised. He had been right. After all. It was no good pretending for the sake of other peoples feelings, even though it was her daughter, when she didn't feel that it was right.

"I'm sorry mother, I shouldn't have rushed you. We've plenty of time, still, you know."

After Jane had left for the studio, Vicky rang Sotheby's and arranged another meeting with Madison Haynes. Then she rang John and thanked him once again for his advice and read out the letter to him that she had received from Sotheby's this morning. "I'm going to see them tomorrow and pick up the ring. I still think that it is Queen Victoria's," she said with a laugh, "or maybe it's because I want to believe that it is hers."

"It is disappointing, but I don't know how they can be absolutely sure that it has nothing to do with Queen Victoria. I would keep an open mind on that." he said. "By the way, I went to the loch where you found it the other day," he said.

"You didn't go looking for treasure, did you?" she teased.

"No, but I've put a few feelers out up at the shooting lodge there. They know me quite well and I said that I would like to write an article on some of the history attached to it and whether they kept a list of all their eminent royal visitors over the years and whether there were any personal stories I could add, like something being lost over the years---maybe in the loch?" She laughed at the nerve of the man, "Weren't they a tiny bit suspicious at this?"

"No, why should they be? I'm always writing about all manner of things to do with Scotland. In fact they seemed rather pleased to be asked. So we will wait and see what comes of it."

"Alright," she said, keep in touch." Vicky thought of John as she made her way across London to Sotheby's again, only this time on her own. It was simply going to be a matter of picking the ring up and going back to Jane's. She remembered to turn around in the strange little lift so that she was facing the right way when it stopped and she wouldn't look foolish, like the last time.

Madison Haynes was sitting elegantly at her desk and she commiserated with Vicky how disappointing it was to all of them that its provenance could not be attributed to Queen Victoria, and how amazing it was to think that the ring must have lain in the loch for well over a hundred forty years and had not been damaged.

"If the crest was not an Imperial one, was their expert in Heraldry able to pinpoint to which European House it did belong?" Vicky asked. Madison Haynes shifted uncomfortably in her chair, "More information would depend," she said, "upon whether Vicky wished to put the ring up for auction----?"

"Oh, no,------ I can't sell it, it doesn't belong to me. I would have to ask my son" Miss Haynes shoulders lifted in an imperceptable shrug as she turned and wrote a number on a piece of card. "Take this downstairs to the auction office to reclaim the ring. Should you change your mind don't hesitate to contact us again." she said standing up and with a charming smile escorted Vicky to the lift.

Vicky handed the card to the man in the office and was given the ring. She slipped it back on her finger and surreptitiously kept on looking at it as she made her way back home. She had been slow, she thought, not to have offered payment for information, but it had all taken her by surprise and she had felt a little confused. Of course they were not going to play ball with her if she was unwilling to put the ring up for auction. How stupid she was. She admired the ring again and knew in her heart that however much money it might make, she could never part with it.

That night at dinner the phone rang. Jane answered it. Her face broke into a smile, "Bruce? hello. We're just having dinner, so can I ring you back?" she suggested. "Oh,-- alright then, Bruce wants to speak to you mother." She handed the phone to Vicky.

"Hello dear?"

"Mum, I know this is something of an imposition but I have business to do in Edinburgh, I cannot put it off any longer and I really need you to come back here to look after Callum, at least for a little while."

"Whatever's happened?" she asked alarmed. "Is Lindsay alright?"

"No, she's not been at all well and she has gone to her mother's, so that she can have a complete rest, so we're in a bit of a mess. I'm sorry about this, but do you think you could come?"

"Yes, of course I will."

Tell Jane I'm sorry about this. Mum, just make the arrangements, let me know and I will pick you up from the airport."

"Yes, alright." She heard the burr of the phone as he put it down. As she replaced the phone, Mark and Jane were looking at her questioningly.

"He wants me to go back there straight away to look after Callum because Lindsay is not well and has gone to her mother's. for a rest."

Are you going?"

"Of course, they need me."

"I'll make the arrangements for you, mother, and we will take you to the airport." Mark said helpfully, getting up from the table.

"Oh, I think that I'd better take the car and drive up." Vicky said.

"Mum it's too far, you would have to break your journey. This is really very inconsiderate of him to expect you to drop everything and drive all that way back on your own."

"He wouldn't have done this if it wasn't urgent, and I don't want to find myself up there without transport if I have to stay for any length of time."

"Do you think she's left him?" Jane asked with narrowed eyes."

"For goodness sake Jane," Mark scolded. "This is not helpful." But as Vicky met her daughter's eyes, she couldn't help but think that only something as dire as that would make Bruce ask for help. Surely if Lindsay was ill, she would have had to go into hospital.

Vicky played with her meal, she had no appetite now as she wondered what disaster would have made Bruce ask her to return. Jane didn't help with her speculations that it must be something to do with Lindsay. She went to her room and packed her bags in readiness for an early start.

*   *   *

CHAPTER EIGHT

It was late when she drove into The Croft. Bruce was waiting for her. Despite his warm embrace and apologies for asking her to come at a moment's notice, he looked tired and drawn. He helped her in with her bags, As Vicky stood in the kitchen she couldn't help but notice how cluttered the kitchen table was with dirty plates and cutlery. She was a little shocked to see half a bottle of whisky standing beside two other empty bottles. He made her a cup of tea, pushing papers out of the way to make a space for it. Then, when they were sitting down he said in a tautly controlled voice,

"My marriage is over, mum. Lindsay has left us." His voice shook and he took a few moments to recover his composure.

"She left me a letter," he went on. "The baby is—is not mine - but Graham's. He has left Morag and they have both disappeared together." He got up and poured himself a large whisky draining the bottle and putting it next to the other empty bottles standing on the table. "I didn't want Jane to know, when I rang up. Callum doesn't know. I've told him that she has gone to her mother's for a rest."

"Oh, my dear, I'm so terribly sorry. When did all this happen?

"She left last week. For the first time in my life, mum, I do not know what to do." He shook his head from side to side. "I feel so utterly helpless, and on top of all this, I have to go to Edinburgh. I cannot put it off any longer. That's why I called you, I need you to be here for Callum."

"Of course, and I will be," she promised.

"Mum, I've left a letter for Lindsay, if she comes back to—to get her belongings. I've put it behind the clock on the mantel piece in the sitting room." he paused, then, "Whatever you may think of her, for my sake and Callum's don't-- please don't make it difficult for her---------Maybe she needs- a little time to think things over--- it is all such a foolish, foolish madness-"----he shrugged helplessly and turned away.

"Of course I won't Bruce," she said steadily, although the pain and anxiety in her heart for him and Callum, smote her. Did this mean that he would take her back she wondered. A quick look around told her that she was indeed needed, but right now she was dropping with weariness and sadness. She put her arms around Bruce and kissed him goodnight before going to her room. Mercifully she was so tired that she slipped into an exhausted deep sleep and was woken up by an exuberant Callum the next morning,

"Daddy said you would come. Mummy's away, she's gone to see grandma Cameron," he informed her smiling happily.

"Yes, and your daddy's got to go away for a few days too, so we shall be left to hold the fort together, won't we?"

They all breakfasted together before Bruce left and she and Callum walked down the long grassy track to the crossroads in the wood to wait for the school bus. Callum had let the labrador, Hamish, out of his kennel to accompany them. Vicky waved him off on the bus before walking back to the house with Hamish who expected to be put back in his kennel enclosure, but Vicky, who could never bear to see any animal caged, left him to his own devices in the yard.

She left the back door open and nearly laughed at the dog's puzzled expression at being left the opportunity to please himself. He looked like an elderly gentleman waiting with perfect manners to be invited in. Probably Bruce would not approve and certainly Lindsay wouldn't, saying that it would lead to a lack of obedience. She didn't care. Lindsay was not here to see. And beside she was a fine one to talk about obedience. What about her marriage vows.

As she washed up she could see Lindsay's mare, Jet, peacefully grazing in the field. The house felt eerily empty as she went from room to room tidying, dusting and vacuuming, restoring the chaos that Bruce had left it in as his world had fallen apart. She put some washing on. Later, she let the hens out and collected their eggs. She looked into Jet's stable. The door had been propped open for her to go into if she wanted to escape the flies and midges. The rest of the stable yard was filled with the plants that Lindsay had left. They had not been watered and were in various stages of decay. She found the hose and watered them. Goodness knows why I'm doing this, she thought!

Back in the house she made a sponge cake and got something out of the freezer for the evening meal. She examined the fridge and calculated when she would have to go shopping for milk and bread. She had no wish to go out and risk meeting someone she knew like Beth or even her friend Jean. At this moment in time she could not answer their questions, No, she wanted to keep a low profile until it all became clearer, in order to protect Callum until he was told by his father or her. Jane rang her and Vicky thought it was wiser to tell her that she knew no more than Bruce had told her------that Lindsay was with her mother, while she took care of Callum. If Bruce was hoping for a reconciliation then it wasn't right to tell Jane what had happened, at least not yet.

"Look after yourself, mum. Give them my love and keep in touch."

In the afternoon Vicky walked down the track with Hamish following at her heels to meet Callum off the school bus. He told her about what he had been doing that day. "What would you like for tea?" she asked him. He ran ahead of her with the dog and shouted back at her, "Egg and chips please." and she thought, Oh, Lindsay, Lindsay, how could you do this to your sweet boy?

Bruce rang most evenings ostensibly to see if they were alright but Vicky sensed his longing for news of Lindsay. She asked him about business and his clients, but underneath it all she could hear the halting unspoken question hovering between them, Had Lindsay returned? He spoke with Callum, asking him about school and whether he was helping grandma with the hens, his mother's horse, Jet, and not to forget to feed Hamish. Like most boys of his age he answered his father's questions in a monosyllabic way but before the call ended, Vicky heard him say, "and I love you too, daddy," before replacing the phone.

Sometimes in the evening after Callum had gone to bed, Vicky wondered tentatively whether she might ring John Brown. He was her friend, after all. Alone up here, she needed a friend to talk things over with, but then, perhaps it wouldn't be right or fair to divulge Bruce's matrimonial troubles to someone who was not family. Now was not the right time, she decided, so that she jumped when her mobile rang unexpectedly as if she had willed it.

"Hello, your majesty. This is your devoted servant Ma'am. enquiring after your well-being?" John's richly timbred voice asked. In spite of herself she giggled. "I'm finding Disraeli and London a little tedious, Brown." she said imperiously.

"I'm not surprised, "he said drily. "Perhaps you need the Highland air, Ma'am."

"It's funny you should mention that, Brown. I would like you to see that my pony is saddled and bridled for me."

"Really Ma'am, and when are we to expect you?"

"I'm closer than you think, John" she laughed.

"Where are you?"

"As the crow flies, about two miles?"

"From where?" he demanded.

"From that place where I trespassed up the glen once.-
---I'm in Scotland, John, at my son's, to look after Callum whilst his parents are away."

"Oh, that's wonderful Vicky, when can we meet?"

"Well, I'm free most days after I've seen Callum off on the school bus."

"Have you got your car?"

"Yes, but I don't know how to get to your place by car. Remember I came trespassing through the woods."

"Of course you did. I will come and get you about eleven tomorrow." She gave him directions, "When you get into woodland, take the first track to your right. The Croft is about half-a-mile on. It's a bit bumpy" she explained.

"That's alright I'll come in the Land Rover. See you tomorrow." When Vicky awoke she was glad to see that it looked like being a fine day. At breakfast Callum seemed quiet and pensive.

"Grandma, do you think mummy will ring me tonight?" Her heart went out to him. He was missing his mother. "Daddy phones but mummy doesn't. Why doesn't she?" he looked at her with his big serious brown eyes.

"I think your mummy is feeling a bit too poorly. I'm sure she's missing you, and would ring you up if she could." He nodded his head. As they walked down the track together to wait for the school bus, he put his hand in hers and asked, "Can we go and get Tweed for me to ride again, grandma?"

"I don't know, we will have to see if the Gilchrists will let us have him." His eyes lit up with their usual sparkle, "Can we go there tonight?"

"We'll see." She waved him off.

Vicky heard the Land Rover as it turned into the yard and came out to meet John. "I haven't been to this little neck of the woods before", he said standing and looking around him at the grey stone stable- block and the gabled farmhouse with its fields stretching beyond to the hills and mountains.

"Would you like to come in and have a coffee, John?"

"No, no, I've got the coffee on, thank you. We'll go if you are ready."

"Yes, I'll just get my jacket." She dashed into the house and back. As he turned the Land Rover around he noticed Jet grazing in the paddock.

"They have a very nice set-up here. Who rides?"

"Oh that's Lindsay's mare."

"What does your Bruce do?"

"He's in the publishing business, but he likes to keep some livestock, a few sheep and some hens. When he was a child we farmed and it sort of gets in the blood."

"What sort of books does he publish?"

"Mainly gun sport, deer-stalking, gun-dog training, hunting, shooting and fishing, countryside, that sort of thing. Oh crumbs," she said startled, "I didn't notice where you turned off, too busy talking," she said, as they drove up a tree lined drive which suddenly opened up into a lawned area with a gravelled circular drive stopping before an imposing turreted gey stone house. "Gosh," she said, "now I really do feel like Queen Victoria."

He laughed, "I inherited it." he said modestly and I have a heck of a job to heat it." Secretly, he was pleased she was impressed. As he drew up, two spaniels and a Gordon setter came running toward them with tails wagging.

"Down," he commanded the dogs as he helped her out, and led her to the side of the house. I always use this door rather than the main entrance, keeps it clean." he explained as they went through a flag-stoned hallway into a large warm kitchen. The dogs followed them in and Vicky stooped to fondle them. "They are enjoying the fuss," he said. "They miss Catriona, my wife." Cups and saucers were laid on the table. He sat her down and went over to the stove. "Do you like black or white Ma'am?" he asked lifting the pot.

"Black please," They sat companionably smiling at each other as they held their coffee.

"I cannot believe this, that you are here with me, right now. His eyes probed hers. What happened to bring you back to Scotland again, so soon ---some emergency?" he asked gently. She looked away and put her cup down. In a flash she thought, he knows. She didn't know what to say. An awkward silence stretched between them.

"I'm sorry," he said. "I didn't mean to sound nosey. I just wondered----"

"You know, don't you----you've heard a rumour?" tears started to well up and course down her cheeks. He took her hands in his and shook his head, his eyes sought hers as she started to cry noisily. The dogs went over to her and worriedly nuzzled her. "Get in your beds," he ordered and they slunk away.

"Vicky, I don't know anything, I've not heard anything. I don't know what you mean. Please Vicky, don't cry." She stood up and he enfolded her shaking frame against him as she buried her head in his jacket and sobbed uncontrollably, all the tensions and emotions of the last few weeks, months, years, poured out of her against her will, making her feel doubly ashamed of this painful outburst before him. He gave her his hanky as she fought to gain control of herself.

"I'm so sorry. I—I didn't want to tell you, and then I thought you knew, and then----I'm sorry--" she sniffled and blew her nose.

"Please don't tell me you've bought that poky flat in Kensington?" She laughed in spite of herself and gave a wry smile. and shook her head.

"That's better," he smiled back. "Well I'm glad it's not that. Come, our coffee has gone cold," He walked over to the sink and threw it away.

"Can I go somewhere and wash my face?" He showed her where to go, "Don't get lost, I'm putting fresh coffee on."

Vicky bathed her ravaged looking face in cold water. Whatever will he think of me, she thought? As she entered the kitchen, she said,

"Oh John, I'm so sorry. I'm so ashamed of myself. I guess it's the tension I am under. The truth is--"

"No, I don't want to know." John cut across her.

"But I want to tell you," she said calmly. "The reason that I am here now looking after Callum, is that there is some trouble between Bruce and Lindsay. She is not around at the moment and Bruce has to be in Edinburgh. Callum, at the moment thinks she has gone to visit her mother."

"And has she?"

"No."

"Do you know where she is?" Vicky lifted her hands and shrugged her shoulders.

"No. It's a mess. She is probably with someone else."

"I see. Oh Vicky, what a burden to carry, I'm so sorry. I understand why you were so upset."

"I haven't mentioned it to anyone else, not even my daughter, in case it can all be smoothed out. It is just a waiting game." He frowned, "Yes, I understand, it won't go any further, and I genuinely have heard no gossip, but then I'm always the last to know anything---- but surely Bruce has to seek a divorce?------ It can't be smoothed out," he reasoned.

"I really can't say----there is Callum, their son, to take into consideration."

"I see," John pulled a face and then took her arm,

"Let me show you around this old house now, come with me." He led her into the main entrance hall, shutting the dogs out. The traditional deer- stalking trophies hung around its grey stone walls. He took her into one of the reception rooms. It had lovely long casement windows down to the floor which faced south and let the sun come streaming in. She looked out onto lawned gardens and beyond that to the mountains. It was a fine view. There was another equally resplendent drawing room and a large oak-panelled dining room with a Jacobean refectory table and chairs for the more formal occasion, The next room, he laughingly referred to was the ballroom, again with long windows which opened out romantically onto a balustraded patio. The next room was much smaller with a wood-burner in an open fireplace. There was a comfy looking leather suite and a television in the corner. A veritable library of books lined its walls. It looked a well-used room. A desk with a stack of paper neatly piled upon it and a computer stood before the window. He smiled, "This is my snug." He waved a hand at the desk, "I'm writing a book at the moment, but every now and again I need to come up for air and get away from it for inspiration."

"What sort of book?" she asked.

"Natural History, That is my subject but, to confine myself inside for hours writing every day is a very hard discipline for me, but it brings in the money," he added. They climbed a central staircase with a solid carved oak balustrade. Oil portraits, of men and women, presumably John's ancestors looked out at them as they passed. At the top of the stairs there was a modern oil painting of a striking looking woman, not unlike Fiona with her piercing ice-blue eyes, except that this woman's eyes were a searching warm brown. Her dark hair was pulled back into a pony-tail tied with a red ribbon. She wore breeches, her hand rested on the head of a Gordon-setter sitting beside her.. Vicky tried not to stare but she wondered whether this was Catriona, John's late wife. She pointed to the setter. Is that the one we have just seen? "she asked.

"Yes, that's Tan—with Catriona, painted six years ago--- before she became ill" he added. Vicky remained silent. What was there to say in the face of death. They both faced the same loss and the understanding of this between themselves, was their unspoken comfort. Next to Catriona was a handsome portrait of John, dressed in an open-necked shirt with a cravat, and tweed jacket, every inch the country gentleman, she thought. They certainly made a handsome pair.

"Up here," he said, moving on. "We have six bedrooms, three with en-suite and one big cold draughty family bathroom." He laughed as he quickly opened and shut doors for her. "Well, that's all up here, but you haven't seen outside yet."

"I'm impressed, John Brown," she said. At the back of the house were beautiful Victorian stables.

"I thought you would appreciate these." he said, "even if they don't have any horses in them at the moment, but that can change."

"Does Fiona ride?" she asked.

"Yes, she's a fine horsewoman, but now she's away she doesn't have the time. The horses are away at livery at the moment." He led her into another huge building which adjoined the stabling and would once have housed carriages but now it housed all sorts of wild life that had met with accidents or man's cruelty and needed hospitalisation but were capable of being restored back into their habitat, from the golden eagle, osprey, buzzards, gosshawk and other hawks. A huge netted enclosure led off the building to make an outdoor flying aviary as the birds progressed. Vicky realized that it was this that she had caught sight of when she had been riding Tweed through their woodland.

"I met your daughter Fiona, one day, with a magnificent eagle on her shoulder. She said she was taking him for a walk."

"Yes, she's very good at helping me when she's at home. I do have a man, James, a full time helper, when we get busy or when I have to go to London, and his wife Marian housekeeps for me. They live in a cottage here in the grounds." He pointed to where she could just make out smoke curling up from a chimney, the cottage lay hidden behind shrubbery.

"We have lots of room for various mammals that we sometimes get brought in, from otters to fox-cubs and badgers and who knows, one day we may even have wolves or bears?" She looked at him to see if he was joking.

"People are already keeping them here on huge fenced estates, and arguing for them to be let out in wild and lonely places to live freely,---to control the deer by natural culling instead of shooting, so, I think it is only a matter of time.

"Where I came from in Wales, many people say that they have seen a black panther or panthers roaming the hills and farmers think that something larger than the fox has taken their sheep. Either someone has let a pet go free that they can no longer manage or they have escaped from one of the wildlife parks." He nodded his head, "Very likely." he agreed.

"Well, I've shown you my estate and something of my work--"

"---and very impressive it is too." she remarked.

"We'll go up to the hotel and get a bite of lunch, before I take you back home. The mountains loomed larger as they drove on down the glen to the hotel which was popular with walkers and climbers in or out of season, so that the hotel remained open all year round. It was a mild day, and they sat outside and ordered a salad and a glass of white wine.

"It has been such an interesting day John, thank you for showing me around your home."

"Vicky, dear Vicky," he said looking closely at her with a warmth in his blue eyes as he took her hand in his, "I can't tell you how much it has meant to me to see you again. I am sorry about the circumstances, but how marvellous that you dropped everything and came, it's so good for Callum too, he added. "I'm here to help you in any way I can, just don't go back to London without letting me know, promise?"

"I promise" she said.. "By the way I may be getting Callum a Highland pony, so we could be riding over one day."

"Splendid, there would be lots for him to see."

"Now, I really ought to be getting back to meet the school bus." she said withdrawing her hand from his as she got up.

"Of course." John went into the hotel to pay the bill while she strolled down to the Land Rover. They drove back in a companionable silence. It felt good. She hadn't felt so relaxed for a long time. At her request he dropped her off at the end of the track where she could meet Callum.

After a phone-call and an early tea, Vicky and Callum set off to together to walk to the Gilchrists farm. Andrew had told Vicky that they still had Tweed and that he would 'suit the wee boy fine." A price had been agreed and Vicky had the cheque in her pocket. What Callum needed at this time was something of his very own to love and to care for and have fun with and Vicky didn't feel she needed Lindsay's permission. By her own actions she had surely forfeited the right.

When they reached the barns, Beth's husband Ivor and their son Andrew, were both there to see Callum's face light up with delight. They had groomed and smartened Tweed up and even oiled his hoofs. The pony peered at them with his large calm eyes through the tangle of his characteristic Rastafarean forelocks. He wore a smart looking leather bridle with a brass headband and was saddled all ready for Callum to ride him back home. When the business was done, Ivor asked her to come down to the house to see Beth but Vicky declined saying that the light was going and they wanted to get back before dark.

"Give my apologies to Beth, I'll see her later." and she swung Callum up onto the saddle adjusted the stirrups for him and told him to hold the reins as she walked Tweed back home.

"Is he really mine, grandma,?"

"Yes, he's all yours to ride and to take care of, your very own friend."

"But, what will mummy say, will she let me keep him?" he asked, obviously worried as he remembered the last time she had wanted to buy Tweed for him.

"I think she will, if you see to his food and his water and groom him. After all your mummy loves horses, doesn't she?"

"I will do all those things, I promise"

"I will help you to begin with, and then it's up to you." Callum enjoyed the rocking motion of Tweed as they walked back home, but he was quite relieved to dismount. He was stiff. It had been far enough for the first time. He threw his arms around the pony's neck, and kissed his nose and told him he loved him. Jet, his mother's horse came flying across the field and both horses whinnied shrilly to each other in recognition.

"There, they've missed each other." Vicky said as she turned Tweed out into the same field as Jet. They stood watching the pair of them as they touched noses and whickered softly before they both dropped their heads and started peaceably to graze together. Callum hugged Vicky, "Thank you grandma, I love him.

"And I love you," she said kissing him. He suddenly thought, "Won't daddy be surprised?"

"Shall we tell him tonight when he phones?" Vicky said.

"Can I?" he asked excitedly. Vicky smiled, it was good to see the child so happy.

"Come on, let's go and see whether the hens have laid us any eggs for tomorrow's breakfast. I didn't have time to go and look this morning." she said a little guiltily. He ran ahead of her and let the waiting hens into the coop whilst Vicky went and filled a pan with feed for them. Callum opened the nest boxes and shouted that they had laid six eggs. He made an apron holding out the ends of his jumper while Vicky laid each one into it. He walked carefully back to the kitchen with them. Vicky ran a bath for Callum, "When you've got your jim-jams on, come downstairs and we'll ring daddy."

* * *

Bruce put the phone down and contemplated the conversation, He smiled at Callum's joy over his grandmother's gift of Tweed to him. He was pleased for him, that his mind was being taken off any anxiety for his mother. He looked around the comfortable but cheerless hotel room and longed to be back home. His publishing business was not going too well. Recession was biting and having its effect on sales. It seemed to him by a cruel stroke of fate, life was dealing him one blow after the other. There was a sick emptiness in the pit of his stomach each day. At night when he returned to the hotel, the emptiness chilled him. Thoughts chased themselves endlessly around his head. Why hadn't he seen all this coming?----and could he have stopped it if he had? The good times had passed both in his business and in his marriage. Even his own mother had sensed that something was wrong and had questioned him. And he, the fool, had laughed,--- laughed, and brushed the misgivings away. Where was Lindsay now? he wondered. He had rung her mobile a thousand times and texted her. Surely things couldn't end as abruptly as this—just to leave a letter for him, the contents so galling to his pride as he thought how surprised and thrilled he had felt over the baby, their baby----he closed his eyes with the sudden stab of pain at the deception---all the deceiving which must have been going on for months,--- it was not his---not his, but another's,---- Graham's! He had thought at the time of seeing it leap off the page at him, how extraordinary that it had not killed him in that instant. Instead, a mind-numbing blankness of unbelief seeped through his mind like a fog, followed by an anger that could have killed. Now, he felt a hopeless depressive nothingness. He had to stay a few more days, and then he would go home to Callum, his son, and try to do his best by him.

CHAPTER NINE

Before the week-end came, Vicky realised that she could not delay shopping any longer. As her car traversed the single track narrow lane out of the glen, she couldn't help glancing at Morag and Graham's place, an old white painted gabled farmhouse with a row of wooden stabling, set down in a sheltered valley not far from the road. A sign indicated the drive to the Market Garden that he ran, the mutual interest that had obviously drawn Graham and Lindsay to each other in the first place. Vicky thought. A movement caught her eye. A man was standing outside the house, smoking a cigarette, he looked up at the road as she drove past. Surely, it was Graham standing there, she thought and then was startled to find that her car had drifted to the other side of the road, Swiftly she corrected it and was past the house before she could look again. She could have stopped but that would have drawn attention to herself. Perhaps on the way back she could quite genuinely stop to see Morag. After all, if her husband had left her for Lindsay, she must be very unhappy and maybe she could tell her what had been going on.

Vicky shopped swiftly, picking up milk, bread, butter, flour, tea, coffee, bacon, some fruit and vegetables and toiletries. her mind still in a whirl as to which option she should take. As she left the shop she heard someone call her name, turning she saw with dismay Beth Gilchrist bearing down upon her. Vicky forced herself to smile.

"My dear," Beth took her arm, "I'm so glad to see you've come back to look after that poor boy, and how kind of you to buy him a pony, you really should have come and had a cup of tea with me the other evening" She dropped her voice, "Has she come back yet?" she asked, her face full of interested concern.

"I'm sorry?" Vicky queried, eye-brows raised as though surprised at the implication, but her heart beat a little faster. Beth, undaunted ploughed on.

"I've heard Graham has gone back to his wife." Vicky hoped she looked mystified as she said, "Oh? I don't know what you mean. Look Beth, you will have to excuse me, I've got to fly", looking at her watch, "or I'll miss the school bus. We'll catch up later". She forced a smile, then ran to her car, started up the engine and shot off with a quick wave to Beth still standing there. Out of sight of Beth, Vicky pulled off the road. She was trembling. If Beth knew, that meant that everybody knew. Where was Lindsay if Graham was back with Morag? She started the car. She had no answers. Yet all these thoughts crowded her head as she drove back. As she passed Morag's place she slowed down to glance at the house to see if she could see Graham but no-one appeared to be about.

Back at The Croft she hurried in with her bags of shopping. A slight movement made her glance up at the stairs. Lindsay was halfway down the stairs carrying a suitcase. They both jumped and then froze at the confrontation. For what seemed an eternity each stood staring at the other. The pale luminosity of Lindsay's face stood out. She looked haunted with deep shadows under her hollowed eyes. Vicky could see that Lindsay now looked obviously pregnant. Lindsay, was the first to recover saying in a small voice, "What are you doing here Vicky?"

"My dear, I'm here to look after Callum, of course," she said sharply.

"I'm sorry.---" An uncomfortable silence followed

"Where's Bruce then?"

"He had to go to Edinburgh."

"Oh.---only I have a letter for him," twisting an envelope over in her hands and staring at it.

"He has left a letter for you too dear," Vicky said in a more conciliatory tone of voice, "behind the clock on the mantelpiece in the sitting room," Vicky indicated, as she walked into the kitchen to put her bags down and fill the kettle and busy herself getting cups and saucers, milk and sugar, to give Lindsay time to read the letter from Bruce in privacy and to still her own anxiety. A few minutes later Lindsay walked into the kitchen and sat down quietly while Vicky bustled about as she put some shopping away before pouring a cup of tea for them both. She sat down opposite Lindsay who took a sip of tea before raising her head and looking steadily at her.

"You know, don't you?" she asked. Vicky leaned toward her. "I know that you may be making a terrible mistake Lindsay that you may live to regret ---and---what about Callum?"

"It's gone too far." Lindsay's eyes brimmed with tears. "I told Bruce that--that it was not his baby."

"Yes, I know----and do you love this Graham?" Lindsay burst into tears and sobbed and spoke incoherently, "I did, but he wanted me---to have an---- abortion---or he would leave me.--- But it was too late for me to ---- I hate him." she added vehemently.

"Where is Graham now? Has he gone back to Morag?" Lindsay nodded, shoulders heaving with another paroxysm.

So, Beth was right about that. Vicky sat quietly until Lindsay's sobbing diminished and then asked,

"Where were you going, with your case, when I came back just now?"

"To er, to my mother's. Graham is coming to take me there." Lindsay explained looking at her watch.

"What, now?"

"Yes."

"Does your mother know about all this?"

"No, not yet"

"Callum has been told that you have gone there to see your mother for a little while because you are poorly.------ Look here Lindsay, you are not the first person to have messed up your life, nor will you be the last. I'm sure that this has been a very painful experience for you and I don't know whether it can be mended. That will be between you and Bruce. He rings up every evening to see if you have come back and have read his letter. I think he is out of his mind with worry. That sounds like love to me."

Lindsay sat grasping the letter, head bowed in shame, so that Vicky was moved to go to her and put her arms around her.

"There is no need for anyone else to know what has happened. They may speculate but they need never know. It's up to you and Bruce. You need to speak together and sort this out."

"I'll phone him and arrange to meet him, that is, if he still wants to see me," she added humbly. Will you stay and look after Callum,?" Vicky nodded. "Of course." She turned toward Lindsay,

"Where did all this start to go wrong?" Lindsay gave a big shuddering sigh, "Graham and I, we were thrown together, through our work.--- I was bored. Bruce was always away Graham paid me attention and---- I thought I loved him." and then in a rush, darting a look at Vicky, she said,

"I never felt that you or Ian thought that I was good enough for your son."

"Oh Lindsay, I'm sorry, my dear, if you thought that. We thought you didn't like us, you --you were so off-hand with us sometimes.----Come, dear, let's put all this behind us and see if we cannot start again without all these hurtful imaginings.?" Vicky stood up and went round to her and embraced her,

"We are family, Lindsay." she said, rocking her now compliant body against hers." There was a knock at the door. Lindsay stiffened.

"That will be Graham." she said getting to her feet and picking up her case. "Thank you Vicky," she said awkwardly, "for looking after Callum."

"There's just one thing, Lindsay, ring Callum up, let him know that you love him, dear."

From the kitchen window Vicky watched Graham put Lindsay's case in the boot of his car, before they drove off together. For a brief instance she saw his face, unsmiling and grim. Vicky shook her head. What a mess!

That evening she had to force herself to be light-hearted with Callum as she gave him another lesson on Tweed. Later, she heard him babbling with happiness as he talked to his father on the phone. She spoke briefly to Bruce,

"I'll ring you back, after I've put Callum to bed, okay?" Vicky left it awhile until she was sure that Callum was sleeping, before ringing Bruce back. "I've seen Lindsay today and spoken with her," she said.

"Yes, I know, she has just phoned me." His voice sounded hollow.

"I'll come home tomorrow, for the weekend. We'll talk then." he said briefly and put the phone down. Vicky's heart went out to him. She could only guess at his distress. In her helplessness she rang John and told him of the development. She felt that he was a little shocked by the revelation of the baby. "That complicates things somewhat," he said, "Surely, they will divorce now. It's an impossible situation for Bruce."

"And a terrible one for her—the disillusionment with her lover letting her down."

"Hmm? Well, yes. He's let her down very badly. The man's a swine. I suppose he's gone back to his wife. It's a bit Thomas Hardy," he said.

"I don't know what Morag, his wife will do."

"Thank goodness you are there Vicky, for Callum and Bruce. You will be busy this weekend, but we'll meet again soon. I'll phone you."

Vicky wondered whether she had said too much to John about their troubles. He obviously found it all very distasteful. At best he had seemed old-fashioned in his views. Had she presumed too much on their friendship, burdening him as well as herself? She couldn't help it, she felt that she needed him as her friend. There was no one else for her to turn to. It all hinged upon the decisions of Bruce and Lindsay. She hoped against hope that Jane would not ring up and enquire about Lindsay yet again. She felt that she could no longer go on prevaricating.

Vicky spent a restless night, only to fall into a heavy sleep in the morning. She was horrified to see what time it was when she woke and surprised that Callum had not come in and woken her. She drew back the curtains and caught sight of him in the field with Tweed and Jet. He must have managed to turn the big key in the lock. And she must have forgotten to bolt the door. Hurriedly she dressed and went to get breakfast. She walked across the yard and leant her arms across the top of the gate into the field. Callum was busy talking to Tweed. She called to him,

"Come on, Callum, the porridge is on, and daddy is coming home today." He came running to her, "Will mummy be with him?" he asked excitedly.

"No, not today. Your mummy is at grandma Cameron's., remember?" His face fell, and he kicked the ground, "When will she come back," he asked scowling up at her. "I want my mummy."

"Yes, I know you do dear," she said gently, then, "I want you to do something for your daddy after breakfast."

"What?" he asked sullenly.

"I want you to ride Tweed down to the big field, where the sheep are, I will let you through the gate. I want you to ride slowly all round the edge of the field and tell me if you see if any are stuck in the hedge or look as though they are lost or poorly, Then I want you to count them all up for me. Can you do that?"

"Phew! that's a lot to do," he said, but he couldn't wait to eat up his porridge and carry out this grown-up task on Tweed, for his daddy. Vicky felt guilty that she hadn't checked on the sheep before now. She hoped there would be no disasters, A stream ran through the land excusing her from the responsibility of seeing that they were watered. Nevertheless she should have checked on them before now. Vicky opened the gate for Callum to ride through. The sheep were curious and started to come running toward them expecting to be fed. Tweed stolidly stood his ground. When he blew down his nose the sheep scattered, making Callum laugh. They set off on their own along the hedge while Vicky walked into the middle of the field to watch them.

She saw one or two sheep who perhaps had been sleeping and were startled by Tweed and Callum, come running away from the hedge to join the main herd. She felt pleased that the pony was steady and not fazed by the unexpected and had not shied and galloped away with Callum which might have frightened him and put him off riding. She strolled over to the stream to meet him coming back. "Well done," she praised them. "Is everything alright?"

"There's nothing stuck or dead," he said matter-of-factly. They each started to count the herd, laughing as they got different numbers or put the other off by counting out aloud. After much counting, eventually their numbers tallied. As they walked back up to the house Vicky realised that in spite of the shadow of Bruce and Lindsay's future hanging over them all, there was the inner knowledge that, away from the noise and pace and sophistication of London, and in the countryside with its simple chores and way of life, she felt at home and was suddenly filled with a deep contentment.

"Look! There's daddy's car." Callum pointed at the car parked in the drive as he struggled to get off Tweed just as Bruce came to the door. He hurled himself at his father who picked him up and hugged and kissed him, while Vicky held the reins until Callum dragged his father over to see his pony. Vicky's heart went out to him as he exclaimed over Tweed. Bruce was making a great effort but his face looked terrible. He went with Callum to take his bridle off and to stable Tweed, while Vicky went inside to make coffee.

"Thank you mum. He is one very happy boy." Bruce said, as he came back in.

"He is missing his mother." she warned him. That evening, after Callum had been read to, and tucked up in bed by his father, Bruce and Vicky dined together.

"Mum, when you rang me after you had spoken with Lindsay, you made it sound as though Lindsay regretted it all------with Graham," Bruce said.

"Yes, that's right. Lindsay said that Graham had wanted her to get an abortion, or he would leave her. It was too late for her to have an abortion, She told me she now hated him, because he was going back to Morag."

"Well," Bruce said, "she spoke to me later, at her mother's, or wherever she was. Something she said made me call on Morag on the way home and she tells me that it is all over between her and Graham. She wants nothing more to do with him. She apparently has thrown him out and wants a divorce."

"What did Lindsay say to you?" Vicky asked.

"That we needed to talk---*to discuss the division of assets and the custody of Callum.*" He banged his fist on the table. "This is not Lindsay talking," he said with a terrible break in his voice. "This is someone else telling her what to say. So, is she back with Graham, cooking all this up to feather their own nest?" and he put his head in his hands. "It is all over, mum. She does not want a reconciliation. I shall see my solicitor on Monday and take advice on how to proceed." He looked at Vicky, "Somehow we have got to tell Callum,---- poor little boy. What is going to happen to us all?---I've dragged you back here from London---"

"Forget that, Bruce. I'm happy to stay here for as long as you both need me." The phone suddenly rang making them both jump with their jangled nerves. Bruce answered, it was Jane pleased at last to speak with her brother. She started sympathetically to ask him if Lindsay was feeling any better. Was she home now?" She was shocked into silence when he said,

"No, My marriage is over. I don't want to talk about it. Mum will explain," he handed the phone over to Vicky and walked out through the door into the blackness of the night.

"Jane, I will have to ring you later when Bruce isn't here." Vicky said. She understood and put the phone down.

The next few days were terrible. Bruce was gloomy and withdrawn. After more questioning from Callum why his mummy hadn't rung him and why was daddy cross with him, it was left to Vicky to explain to Callum that his daddy was sad and not cross. "Sometimes, she said, people don't love each other any more because they have fallen in love with someone else. That's why daddy is sad. Your mummy has fallen in love with uncle Graham and she has gone to live with him," Callum remained with his head down, twisting a piece of straw in his hands as he listened. "Doesn't she love me anymore?" he asked miserably.

"Of course your mummy loves you and always will, and your daddy too, they will never stop loving you, and you will live here with daddy, and visit your mummy often. You will have two homes."

"When, when will I see her?" he asked, looking up at her.

"Your daddy and mummy will have to arrange that, but hopefully it will be soon." Callum was silent, then, "Will it be like Robert Spencer, in my class? He visits his mummy and a new daddy for weekends and holidays."

"Yes, it will be just like that." She put her arms around him and hugged him, kissing the top of his head, as she thought sadly that divorce was becoming an all too familiar pattern in children's lives today. She hoped that the inevitable mixed loyalties of two homes would not be too damaging to him. "It will soon be the school holidays and Henry and William, your cousins will be coming to see you. So, we will have to think of some nice thing we can do with them won't we? "Vicky said brightly.

* * *

CHAPTER TEN

Vicky stood back in the shadow of the dark green velvet curtains of the drawing room at Ordie House. She looked out onto the sunlit lawn. What had attracted her attention was Fiona, home on vacation. She called to John to join her. Together they watched Fiona walking across the lawn with Callum. Suddenly she scooped him up around the waist and swung him around and around in her arms, her golden Pre-Raphaelite hair streaming out behind her. Callum's legs whirling higher and higher off the ground whooping and laughing uncontrollably until he begged for mercy and they both fell over in a tangle helpless on the ground. Seeing them, Vicky couldn't help smiling at the way Fiona played with Callum, bringing fun and laughter into his life again,

It was as though he was a fond younger brother. Fiona jumped up and held out her hand to help Callum to his feet. Still holding hands together they walked off out of sight around the house toward the stables.

"She's good for him," isn't she? John said to Vicky.

"Very good.." Vicky agreed. It was true that her befriending of Callum had eased things for him. He had confided in Fiona how he wanted his mummy, so Fiona would console him out of her own grief for her mother.

"I miss my mummy too," she told him, "but you will see your mummy again and stay with her for holidays and weekends but I won't ever see my mother again." Callum thought about this.

"Doesn't she love you anymore?" he asked.

"My mother died and so I can't see her." she said simply.

"Why did she die?"

"She became ill, but all mothers never stop loving their children." He nodded. It felt good that he and Fiona shared their secrets, somehow it all felt better because he knew that he could ask Fiona anything and they talked together like grown-ups.

Vicky was aware as they had watched Callum with Fiona, that John had slipped his arm around her shoulders. She went to turn away and he held her closely turning her toward him. His blue eyes always so warm and full of humour were tender and serious, as they sought hers.

"Dear, dear Vicky. Do you know that ---that your coming into my life means everything to me?---but everything.----that I love you to distraction and always will. I need you. Please say that you feel something for me too?" he pleaded. Part of her wanted to throw caution to the wind and say, yes, John, I love you. Instead the words struggled out. "Dear John, this is too soon---We haven't known each other very long, besides there is too much going on---I can't commit to anything at this moment, what with Bruce and looking after Callum ---" She put her hand on his arm. "It is our loneliness, our bereavements---John. We're too old for this—this---madness." She shrugged her shoulders. "What would our families think?" Vicky had a vision of Jane's disapproving face, and Fiona's icy wrath descending on them.

"Can't we remain just good friends for now, John?" she pleaded.

"No." he said, in a tortured voice. He held her face between his hands,

"Vicky, my Royal Vicky, I love you," he murmured. They drew apart a little guiltily as Fiona followed by Callum suddenly came in. She looked from one to the other, "Oh, there you are. We wondered where you were," she said frowning. She knew instantly that she had interrupted something. "We can have tea now, out on the lawn. It's such a lovely day and Bruce has just come. Callum and I have laid it all out."

Like guilty children they followed Fiona and Callum out into the sunny summer day where tea had been laid under the Cedar tree for shade.

More and more often, she and Callum had been invited up to the house. Now, Bruce had become a frequent visitor too. Vicky remembered how Bruce had said that he didn't know Fiona, yet she had mentioned him at their first meeting but when she had asked if Fiona knew him, she had just given an enigmatic smile but had not replied to her question. Bruce, over the weeks had been still too wrapped up in his troubles to notice her and spoke with John rather than to Fiona, but Vicky hadn't failed to notice how Fiona looked at Bruce, hanging on his every word and even flirting a little outrageously with him. John too had noticed and had expressed some misgivings about her, saying that she was infatuated with Bruce who was much too old for her and the sooner she went back to University the better. Vicky thought of them all as having lost someone precious and yet life moves on and brings other people into your life, other joys that you could never have imagined before.

Looking around her as they sat in the garden, Vicky thought that they looked like a perfect family without any troubles. Callum sat on Bruce's lap, Fiona beside him, laughing and talking quietly together, beginning to know each other as friends. Bruce looked relaxed as though his burden of sorrow was forgotten in this moment of time. John sat opposite her looking at her with his warm blue eyes in a certain way, so that she felt a little discomfited. Callum slid off his father's lap and went and stood behind Fiona and started to dreamily plait her long hair. She made it easier for him and lay back smiling with her eyes closed, her long hair hanging over the back of the chair. If only we could all stay like this locked into a time of pure peace and happiness, she thought.

*   *   *

Vicky decided that she would make herself scarce today, when Lindsay was coming to see Callum, and to talk things over with Bruce. She had no wish to be in the way. She guessed that the baby's birth must now be imminent. It would be good for Callum to have his mother's attention before she became busy with a new baby. She felt that Bruce was resigned now to the inevitable but her heart was heavy for Callum and his feelings of divided loyalty between his parents as he met with his mother again. She gave him a kiss and a hug before she drove away.

As soon as Callum heard his mother's car, he dashed out of the house and would have flung himself into her outstretched arms but was stopped by the strange immense shape of her, making it an impossibility for him. She stooped awkwardly to kiss him.

"Callum, baby, I love you darling." He didn't like being called baby but replied dutifully, "I love you too, mummy." Lindsay looked around her, "Where's my horse Jet?" she asked him.

"Oh, grandma put her in the stable so that you could see her. Come on I'll show my pony too," he said holding her hand and tugging at her.

"No, not just yet", she restrained him. "Where's your daddy?" He looked over at the farmhouse. "In there, waiting for you".

"And where's grandma?" she asked cautiously.

"She's gone out for the day, shopping, I think, um, Aberdeen. She said to give you her love." he said suddenly remembering. Bruce stood in the doorway waiting for them to come in. He wanted Callum to enjoy his mother's visit, however bitter-sweet it was for him to see Lindsay again and so heavily pregnant. He had made some tea and they chatted amicably together for a while. Callum became bored and went outside to play with Hamish.

"When is the child due?" Bruce asked. She lowered her eyes, "Three weeks."

"Are you living with Graham?"

"She nodded without looking up." This was painful, he thought, like pulling teeth. "Do you love him, Lindsay?"

"Yes." She looked up at him almost defiantly.

"Is he good to you?"

"Of course." in clipped tones.

"Do you still want this divorce?" She met his eyes.

"Yes, I do. And I want residency rights for Callum, --- with visiting rights for you, of course," she added magnanimously.

"I will not allow you to take my boy from me Lindsay. You've disappeared for weeks on end, without once getting in touch with him. I hope you have enough money, because I shall fight you every inch of the way, believe me." His voice remained quiet but steely in its emphasis, while inside a sinking turmoil raged. She appeared to ignore him and said haughtily,

"I will send a horse-box for Jet next week. "I shall sell her at the next market," said without any emotion in her voice. "Tell your mother also, that I cannot keep the pony she has seen fit to buy Callum."

"No, but I will, and I'm willing to give you a fair price to keep Jet too."

"That is if you can afford to keep this place on, when we halve all the assets, including your business," she said delivering her trump card. He stared at her, dismayed. He did not know her any longer. She was not the woman he had married. He knew in that instant that they could never go back. She got up saying that she would take Callum out for lunch and return him later that afternoon. Bruce with bile in his mouth watched Callum as he got happily into her car waving at him as she drove him away.

Vicky arrived back to find Bruce gloomy and depressed as he recounted his conversation with Lindsay. "I put nothing past that woman." he said bitterly as he recounted their conversation about wanting residency rights. Vicky felt dismay and concern. Together with Bruce they kept on looking through the window waiting for Lindsay's car to appear until suddenly Vicky saw the small figure of Callum walking toward them down the drive, on his own. They rushed out to meet him.

"Mummy dropped me off at the top of the drive," he explained.

"Did you have a nice time?"

"Yes, we went for lunch and then she took me to her new flat. It wasn't in the country and she said I was going to live there too." he said puzzled, looking up at them. "She showed me my bedroom and it was full of toys and stuff. But there wasn't anywhere to keep Tweed. I didn't like it." Bruce and Vicky exchanged looks.

"I told her that I had got to look after Tweed, and—and she said, We'll see. She said, you would take me there next time daddy." Bruce muttered something under his breath while Vicky took Callum upstairs for a bath. Bruce picked up the phone to speak to his solicitor again.

CHAPTER ELEVEN

Jane unfurled her long legs out of the Range Rover as the boys, Henry and William tumbled out looking sleepy and tired from the long journey. Mark opened the back and was getting the luggage out, as Vicky, Bruce and Callum came to greet them, Jane looked at her watch,

"It's taken us eleven long hours mum," They hugged and kissed each other.

"I know, my dears, come along in, there's a meal all ready." By the time Mark had carried their cases in, the boys had disappeared with Callum into the stables.

"Leave them for a while to kick their heels after the long journey." Vicky advised.

"Hi brov.how are you?" Jane embraced her brother looking up into his face trying to gauge his feelings.

"Oh, I'm alright." he said, sweeping aside any allusion to emotion. He disentangled himself from her. "I'll help Mark with the bags."

Jane looked around her before going in, she could hear the boys voices coming from the stables. The sun was beginning to set in a golden glory behind the darkening mountains. She had to admit it was very beautiful and so quiet compared to the ceaseless buzz of London. It would be good to unwind here for a week or two. She hadn't wanted to come to Scotland for the boys holidays. They usually rented a house in the French Pyrenees, but after her mother's phone call saying that it would be a help at this time for the family to close ranks around Bruce as he was going through his divorce, she and Mark had decided that they would all come, It was the right thing to do. Poor things, It must be absolutely ghastly for them. She strolled over to the stables The boys were in Tweed's stable. They surrounded him admiringly.

"Look mum," said Henry, "look at his mane and forelock," laughingly picking up Tweed's long Rastafarean locks, to show her. "He's got ringlets. We're going to ride him tomorrow."

"Come on boys, grandma has got a nice meal for us." They gave Tweed a final pat before reluctantly leaving him. The novelty of the pony had broken the ice between the boys, who hadn't met for two years and the three of them chatted happily as they sat at table with Callum telling them of all the exciting things he had in store for them. The grown-ups smiled indulgently as he laid out the fishing, camping, climbing, riding and exploring trips.

"And then,--- we can go up to the big house" Callum said with pride.

"Oh, and where's that?" asked William.

"It's where grandma and I go---to see uncle John." Jane looked sharply across at her mother and Vicky found herself quite maddeningly blushing as she felt Jane and the boys eyes were on her waiting for a further explanation. Bruce came to her rescue,

"Oh, it's mother's friend, John Brown's place. Yes, it is imposing but the boys will like it for the birds of prey there and the animals he rescues. John is a professor of natural history, you know, and he also has a charming daughter, Fiona, whom you have met I believe, when they were in London?" he said with a questioning smile at Jane, remembering her acute anxiety about the man when she had phoned him about their mother. In the silence that followed Callum added in a serious voice, "Fiona is my best friend too."

"You never told me that he was a professor." Jane said looking at her mother. Vicky looked across at her daughter, "and that would have made all the difference, would it?" she asked with a little smile on her face. Mark said quietly, "Touche."

*   *   *

Together with Bruce, Mark and Jane threw themselves into being part of whatever had been planned for the boys holiday together. Today, Tweed was used as a pack pony to carry their camping gear, where optimistically they were to cook and eat trout from the loch where they fished. Nevertheless Vicky was to bring more substantial fare to them by car in case the fish proved elusive and they starved. It was a beautiful summer's day as they trekked along the valley skirting the mountains. In some places the path narrowed with rocky outcrops and they had to walk in single file with Callum enthusiastically leading Tweed for he knew the way having camped here several times with his father.

Jane stepped carefully, a turned ankle was the last thing she wanted, but she was no stranger to arduous physical exercise. Henry and William took it in turns to lead Tweed, Bruce and Mark with bulging haversacks and carrying a canoe between them, brought up the rear talking together, until they rounded the rocky slopes of a steep vertical mountain to behold the waters of a small sparkling lochan, hidden and secretive before them. They stood entranced by the scene before them and Jane thought, no wonder Bruce never wanted to leave Scotland. She could understand it now, the beauty and silence of these lonely places.

Bruce took charge, giving the boys jobs to do, getting dried fire-wood whilst he and Mark put the tents up. Tweed, still with his halter on and a rope dangling from it, was given his freedom after he had been unpacked, to graze and nibble the heather. Jane sorted out the ground sheets, sleeping bags, cooking pans, fly rods, and water carriers.

Later in the afternoon Vicky left her car at the nearest point and hiked over with eggs, bacon, sausages and bread. Jane came and met her, to carry it to the site where they set to, cooking a supper for them all before Jane and Vicky returned to the farmhouse by car leaving Mark, Bruce and the boys to enjoy their camping adventures together for the next three days.

Once back at the farmhouse Jane and her mother flopped into comfortable armchairs after their exertions of the day. They were enjoying a cup of tea when Jane asked, "Mum, supposing Bruce doesn't get sole custody or residency, as they say in Scotland, and Callum goes to live with his mother, what will you do? Will you come back to us, to London?" Vicky sighed, "We shall have to wait and see what happens. I must say I haven't thought beyond Bruce's latest appeal, I have to support him"

"Mum, he's only going to get residency for him if he can prove that there is someone here permanently to look after him, like yourself."

"Yes, I suppose so."

"And you would be prepared to do that?"

"Of course, he's my son and my grandson, my family in need dear." Jane nodded in understanding and fell silent, while a thousand thoughts whirled around her head, then "Would it be a good thing, do you think, if we took Callum back with us for the rest of his holidays. Show him the sights of London. The boys would like that. They all get on so well, and it would take him out of this atmosphere of Bruce going off to court and all the tensions of that, What do you think, shall we ask Bruce when they get back?

"Yes, but get him on his own first, without the boys." Vicky advised. Because it was so warm, Vicky had left the farmhouse door open. Someone suddenly knocked loudly on it. "Come in." Vicky shouted, and in strode John with Fiona. "Goodness, we didn't hear a car," said Vicky getting to her feet.

"No, we left it at the top of the drive." She turned to Jane, "Of course, you met my daughter Jane.."

"Ah, the ballet dancer," John beamed at her, taking her hand, "You remember my daughter," indicating Fiona who smiled and said, "Hello."

"Well, where are they all?" John enquired, looking around him.

"They are all down at the wee lochan, camping for the next three days."

"Oh, lovely," said Fiona. "Can we go and see them?"

"Too late now, maybe tomorrow---only I can't go," John said.

"I'll go with you tomorrow, if you like Fiona." Jane offered. "I could do with the exercise."

"Okay, I'll come about nine and we'll walk there?" Jane nodded in agreement.

"Now," John said, "What we really came about, was to ask you all to come up to Ordie House for the day, some time next week, and stay to dinner?"

"Oh John, thank you so much, we would love to." Vicky said grasping his hands in a quite familiar way, Jane thought, looking swiftly at Fiona to see what her reaction was. This time Fiona stood there, her face inscrutable. Perhaps their respective parent's behaviour had become an accepted given, Jane thought. After John and Fiona declined any refreshment, Vicky and Jane walked back up the drive with them. At one point John leaned over and whispered something to Vicky. She looked up at him questioningly and he laughed, "I'll tell you later." he said, kissing her lightly on the cheek before getting in the Land Rover and waving goodbye to them. Jane had stiffened at this obvious intimacy in front of both her and Fiona.

The next morning Jane had breakfasted, and was ready and waiting with her walking boots on by the time Fiona arrived. Jane noted that her wild golden locks were tamed and tied back in a pony-tail. They set off together each carrying a light haversack with a packed lunch and a bottle of juice and a fleece should the weather turn chilly. They chatted lightly together, Jane told her what a ghastly journey it had been from London. Fiona talked about her final year at Uni there and that she travelled back and forth to London always by rail or plane. "It's so relaxing. I love train journeys. You see so much more than by car. You look in everybody's back garden, their kitchens and dining rooms, "she laughed self-consciously. "I guess I'm just nosey."

"How do you think Bruce will take it if he loses residency for Callum?" Jane asked her changing the subject.

"He will be totally devastated." Fiona said. "I can't bear to think of it and poor Callum----I love that boy-----That woman Lindsay is disgusting." she added.

"Yes, I'm afraid we never got on." Jane admitted.

"She's killing him." Fiona said dramatically and to Jane's dismay, she started to cry. This was not the ice-maiden whose reputation had gone before her, but someone vulnerable to her brother's pain. Why? Jane wondered. Fiona soon pulled herself together. She was cross with herself for revealing her feelings. They sat down on some rocks to have a drink and for Fiona to compose herself, blow her nose and wipe away her tears.

"Your brother is such a nice person and a good father too, he doesn't deserve this," she explained a little lamely.

"No, he doesn't."

"I used to come across them in Graham's car up the glen, off the road, when I was out riding. I knew what they were up to and I used to crack my whip hard across the roof of the car," she added with a grin. Jane in spite of herself couldn't help but smile too, at this picture of righteous indignation being expressed by this slip of a girl. Fiona went on, "I'm seriously worried Jane, that she is going to fight Bruce all the way for Callum until she has beggared him of every penny." Jane suddenly realized that Fiona must be her brother's confidante. She looked at Fiona with new eyes----interesting, she mused to herself.

"I'm worried that my mother will feel obliged to stay here for Bruce to get residency of Callum."

"Ummm?" Fiona murmured non-committedly. They stood up and adjusted their haversacks on their backs before continuing. She was her father's daughter, pointing out to Jane tracks made by some tiny creature, or deer slots imprinted on soft ground, studying otter spraints, informing her of the height and names of various mountains surrounding them, or a particular hawk flying in the sky. Jane began to look around her with new eyes. In one way or another the whole morning was turning out to be revelatory, she thought.

When they arrived at the camp site beside the lochan, it was deserted. There was only Tweed to whinny a welcome. He was tethered safely away from their tents and food and soon relaxed back into a napping mode in the sun, with his eyes closed, resting a hind leg. The canoe was beached, so

Fiona thought that maybe they were climbing one of the mountains. She cupped her hands around her mouth and suddenly let out an ear-splitting cry, reminding Jane of the 'away' cry in fox-hunting that she had heard once when out cubbing with her mother as a child. It was both chilling and eerie, and somehow belied the feminine instincts of nurture, making the hairs rise on her back. It had put her off fox-hunting for ever. Tweed also had woken up at the banshee scream and shied away clattering the stones beneath his feet, his ears laid back in fright but thankfully the tether held him. Jane started to say something but Fiona shushed her into silence holding up her hand for her to be quiet.. As they waited, in the distance, a similar cry came back.

"Good," Fiona smiled, "I know where they are. Come on, that was Callum, I taught him that." she said pleased with herself. They started to climb. Jane could only wonder if her brother knew what he was taking on with Fiona. She liked her, but there was something a bit formidable about her. She didn't doubt for one minute that they would find them. And so they did, after an arduous climb they met the boys coming to meet them. Fiona put her arm around Callum as they walked back with them. Henry and William tried to outdo one another in relating to their mother all the things they had been doing, until they came to where Bruce and Mark were.

"Can we all have a long sit-down and picnic," Jane pleaded, flopping down on the ground beside Mark, after she had introduced him to Fiona, who went and sat beside Bruce with the same easy familiarity she had shown with Callum.

* * *

LONDON 1876

The people grew restless without their Queen. What was she doing all this time in Scotland? Rumours were being spoken of her and her servant John Brown, There was even talk of a secret marriage between them, and that the queen wore John Brown's mother's wedding ring. It was well known that the 'family' disliked the man. He was getting above himself as a servant. There were even rumours of blackmail over compromising love-letters between the Queen and John Brown.

CHAPTER TWELVE

As the car swept up the drive to Ordie House and it was revealed in all its grandeur, Jane gasped and said to her mother.

"Are they really related to, *the John Brown?*"

"I'm not sure because we always joke about it."

"You mean to say that you haven't actually asked him?"

"No." Vicky sounded amused.

"Mind you, he was only a servant, so the family wouldn't have had any money, would they? And he died a bachelor."

"I'm sure with a name like Brown there must have been many offshoots to the family." Vicky said, still amused at Jane's surmising,

"By the way, did I tell you that Fiona's mother was a Ponsonby."

"Oh, my God! Now that was an important family connected with Queen Victoria"

"Really?" asked Vicky innocently, but the irony was lost on Jane. As the car stopped, John and Fiona and the dogs came to greet them. Fiona kissed Vicky and Jane before saying, "Come on boys, we'll put the dogs in the kennels while I take you to see our birds of prey and then all the animals we rescue and look after.

"We'll see you later for tea," she smiled at them before heading off with the three boys and the dogs across the lawned gardens.

Vicky looked at Fiona's retreating back and smiled. She seemed such a different girl from the one that confronted her at their first meeting. The boys all loved her. Perhaps I've given her back the family she was missing, she thought. Even Jane seemed impressed with her.

"We'll take tea in the drawing room." John said leading the way. Marian, John's housekeeper brought in the tea and cakes,

"Och, Miss Fiona and the wee boys are with James, are they? I'll bring some lemonade and more cakes for them, don't you worry." she said beaming at them all.

"Thank you Marian."

"Shall I pour, Sir, or will Madam?" looking at Vicky.

"We can manage, thank you," he said "We shall be quite a party when Fiona comes in with the boys. It is like a grand family re-union," he beamed.

"In a grand family home." Vicky said, pouring the tea. "Thank you for inviting us John."

"No, no, no. Thank you all for your friendship." he said simply. "Fiona and I appreciate it." Henry and William came running in with Callum.

"Oh, mum, dad, you've got to come and see, they pleaded.

"Alright, in a minute when we've finished our tea." Marian came bustling in with lemonade for the boys and some more 'wee' cakes. They sat and devoured the cakes and lemonade, in-between telling them that they had seen the birds of prey being fed by Fiona with cut-up little chicks and mice and rats. They giggled when they saw their mother's face.

"Do you mind not being so graphic in the details while we are eating," Mark laughingly scolded, before they excused themselves and followed the boys outside.

Once they were on their own, Vicky asked John what was the news he had for her that he hadn't disclosed the other evening when he had called on her and Jane.

"Well, firstly--"

"You mean you've two lots of news?"

"Well, yes,--- patience,--" he said holding up his hand.

"Firstly, I've had a reply from the shooting lodge. The factor who keeps the estates records and the guest books that once belonged to the castle has looked into the records of its illustrious guests for anything lost during their stay and he found recorded that at some time during the Queen's visit, accompanied by her personal servant John Brown, it was noted that Queen Victoria was thought to have lost a mourning ring in memory of HRH Prince Albert, bearing the crest of the House of Saxe-Coburg and Gotha. It was thought that her Majesty might have lost it while painting near the loch. A search was organized, but nothing was ever found."

"Oh, my goodness" Vicky was bowled over by the news."

"Now, you only have to have the crest confirmed as the House of Saxe Coburg and you have its provenance." he said putting the letter into her hands. "You realize it could sell for a lot of money, don't you?" She looked up at him. "This is such exciting news John, but I can't sell it. It isn't mine, Bruce found it."

"Will you tell him?"

"Well, yes, I don't see why not?"

"And---what if he wants to sell it?"

"Ah, well, he did give it to me until my death, when it will rightfully return to him." she said matter-of-factly. He smiled, "Oh Vicky, that's a relief."

"I doubt if anything can top that news so what's the second bit of news? she asked.

"Well," he said with a broad smile, "I've been invited to go to America to study the release of wolves into a large tract of uninhabited land in Yellowstone Park in North America.." Vicky's eyes widened with excitement at the thought.----"and" he went on,---"and, I want you to come with me as my wife, dearest Vicky, because I love you and I can't live without you. So, yes, this is a proposal. Please say, yes---" He stopped and searched her face anxiously--- -"and then we can tell the whole family while we are here all together."

"Oh, John, how can I desert Bruce and Callum at this time when they need me,---- I can't my dear." He saw the pain in her face.

"We can wait,--- can't we?" He looked at her a little sadly, "Vicky, we're too old for this waiting game, aren't we?" She didn't reply, and he said quickly,

"Yes, I know, of course we can. I am a selfish bastard. I wanted you to come with me to America to share the experience, "he paused,

"I may be gone for quite a while," he said, the corners of his mouth crinkling into a smile as he said the famous quote from Captain Scott's diary of the doomed Antarctic Expedition. She couldn't help but smile at him. He was kind, loving and funny. There was no doubt that she would miss him dreadfully, but she could do no other. He put his arms around her and gently kissed her upturned face. To dispel their sadness he said,

"Come on, let's go and see what the others are up to." They walked to where the animals and the birds were kept. James, having fed and watered them was just locking up. "They have all gone for a walk with Miss Fiona and the dogs," he told them pointing in the direction he had seen them go. They strolled slowly, reluctant almost, to catch them up. He held her hand until they reached the woods where the path was narrow.

"This is where I first met Fiona," she said looking back at John. He nodded, "Yes, I know. I was furious with her that I had missed seeing you."

"Do you think she would feel the same about me if she knew about us?"

"I would think that she has already sussed out our relationship, don't you? Besides, I think she has other things on her mind at the moment, to worry about us."

"Do you mean Bruce?" He nodded.

"Yes, it is obvious to me that the girl adores him and would fight his cause for him if she could, but I don't think Bruce has even noticed her, thank goodness. I like Bruce but he's too old for her and then there is all this trouble with his family life. It's much too messy," he said, pulling a face. Vicky felt affronted, "Some marriages do go through difficult messy times, John. Relationships can break down. Life is like that. It has it's disappointments. People can let you down. Would you feel the need to vet all your friends as to their suitability, surely some of them have messed up?"

When it comes to my daughter's future, yes," he said a little testily.

"And have you vetted me John, for my suitability for marriage to you?" she asked. "I might have all sorts of hidden baggage." She stopped and turned to face him with raised questioning brows.

"Don't be silly--" he started to say, but before either of them could say anything else, the boys came crashing through the undergrowth with the dogs.

Dinner that evening around the long oak table in the panelled room was served to them by the husband and wife team, Marian and James.

"We thought we could show you this evening, "John said to Mark and Jane, "how well we live off the land in Scotland." There was a smoked salmon starter, followed by a haunch of venison with a red-currant sauce, and roasted vegetables followed by the best raspberries from Blairgowrie. John looked around the full table and felt quite emotional. If Vicky were to marry him, these dear people would all be his family. After the bleakness of the last few years, sitting in the kitchen, eating alone, when Fiona was away in London, he couldn't believe his luck in meeting Vicky. Jane watched her mother, sitting beside the 'Laird' as she had nick-named him in her mind and Miss Fiona, beside Bruce. She could feel the chemistry. Both couples were living in their own little world, oblivious to anyone else. Yet it was all quite obvious even to a casual observer Jane thought, that both couples were in love. She made an effort to talk to Mark. It was all quite bizarre. When they were back home and the boys had bathed and gone to bed, she teased her mother unmercifully, "Shall I pour Sir, or will Madam?" Vicky smiled but kept silent.

*   *   *

Bruce, in the end agreed to Jane's invitation to take Callum back to London with them for the rest of his summer holidays. At first he had been unwilling in case the Family Court needed to see Callum, but the case had been put back until Lindsay had delivered the child and could attend court herself.

"God knows how long all this is going to drag on." he despaired.

The boys were delighted at the prospect of taking their cousin back with them to experience the sights of London. Callum was excited too. He had never left Scotland. He was looking forward to this big adventure with his cousins. He could hardly wait. Grandma said that she would take care of Tweed for him, and Fiona had told him that when she went back to Uni in London, she would call and see them. And so it was arranged.

Vicky and Bruce, together with John and Fiona waved them all off until they were out of sight. As they returned to the farmhouse, John said to Vicky out of earshot of Bruce and Fiona who had gone on ahead chatting together,

"Well, now that you are minus your young charge Callum for a while, perhaps we can have a little more time together before I depart to America." Vicky looked up at him and smiled, "Yes, that would be nice," and then a little sadly, "it is going to be awfully quiet for us when you have gone and Fiona too will soon be going back to London for her last year won't she?"

"Yes, but I'm glad she has met your family now and has friends in London that she can turn to if she needs them when I am away. She wants her horses back from livery when she comes home again for Christmas and she has been busy clearing the old hay and straw out of one barn to make room for new hay and straw. It's been a good year for it, so it's a good buy right now for the autumn. She's a wonderful girl, really puts her back into it-----wouldn't let James help her. It took her two days. You will be able to ride out with her too, and Bruce, if he wants to."

"Thank you, let's hope the divorce goes through and that Callum will be able to stay with his father. The case seems to be dragging on so."

"Yes, it must be awful for them all." John agreed, calling for Fiona to come and get in the Land Rover. He turned to Vicky and kissed her goodbye. Fiona and Bruce appeared out of the farmhouse. She gave Bruce a peck on the cheek before they drove away.

After John and Fiona left, a terrible emptiness seemed to engulf the place. No prattle from Callum and the boys, no closeness of being able to talk things out as only a close-knit family can. The fun and sharing of the last two weeks with Mark and Jane culminating in a splendid day at Ordie House with Fiona and John only seemed to emphasize the wretchedness of Bruce's life if he lost Callum. For the past two weeks he had put it out of his mind, but now the blackness was coming back.

Vicky set about changing the bed linen and putting the washing machine on. There was really a lot to do. She mustn't daydream about John, and how wonderful it would be if she and John could have shared the American trip together. She sighed. She must get on.

They both heard the police siren in the distance, getting nearer and nearer and both thought, there's been an accident or a fire somewhere. Vicky looked at her watch. They should have made good time by now. It couldn't be them. The siren got louder and then they saw the police car coming slowly down the drive toward them. The siren was turned off and two officers got out of the car. Bruce was white and Vicky felt her legs turn to jelly. "Mr Bruce Lewis? the officer asked, ignoring Vicky. "Could we go inside please Sir?"

"Yes," Bruce said, his heart in his mouth, he looked back to see the other officer walking around the Land Rover, examining it.

"Are those both your vehicles? "the one asked Bruce.

"The car is my mother's." The other officer followed them in shortly. Vicky said, in a distraught voice,

"Please tell me it's not my daughter, and her husband and the boys--- in the Range Rover?" she said fearfully---"

They've been gone an hour?------They haven't had an accident, have they?" Their faces remained impassive.

"My business is with you, Mr. Lewis. It is to do with your wife, a Mrs Lindsay Lewis?"

"Oh?--- yes, but we are in the process of a divorce. She no longer lives here."

"I see. I am to take you back to the station for questioning, sir. Please come with me." He nodded to Vicky, "I'm sorry if I caused you unnecessary anxiety, madam," as Bruce went to get his jacket.

"But what has happened?" she asked him."

"I am not at liberty to say, Is this your son?" as Bruce returned.

"Yes, he is."

"He will let you know, in due course." Vicky followed them out to the car and watched it disappear up the drive with Bruce inside. She suddenly didn't know what to do. Bruce had looked as helpless as she now felt. She hadn't even asked where they were taking him, Dundee or Aberdeen? she didn't know and all she could do was wait.

Bruce was taken to the police station in Aberdeen and put into a room and told to wait. It was one of those situations when you don't know what you are supposed to have done, but you start to feel guilty. He sat down and tried to look calm and relaxed, but inevitably he started to wonder. What trick was Lindsay playing on him now, in order to sway the court? he thought.

Suddenly, the door was opened by a stern-faced middle-aged man with short iron-grey hair. He carried a file in his hand and put it on the desk before introducing himself as Detective Inspector Mike Greig. He sat down, opened his file, looked at it briefly, before fixing him with a stare.

"I'm very sorry to say sir, but your wife was found dead this morning," he paused when he heard the gasp of Bruce's indrawn breath.

"Are you alright sir?" Bruce nodded, but he felt as though all his breath had been sucked out of him

"It looks as if she had been forced off the road by another vehicle which didn't stop or report the accident. Your wife's car had fallen into a deep culvert full of water, and had lain hidden and undiscovered for several days.

"No!----And the baby?" Bruce asked, shocked at this new revelation.

"They are both gone, I am sorry to say. Your wife drowned."

"I would like you to come with me for the purpose of identification, please." and he led Bruce through corridors to the mortuary where the body lay covered in a sheet. An attendant pulled back the sheet to reveal the horribly swollen blue marble-like face of Lindsay. Bruce had gone white with shock. He nodded. "Yes, it is her."

"Would you like a few moments?" Mike Greig asked. Bruce shook his head, There was nothing left to say. They walked back in silence to the room he had been taken to, and sat down, his legs suddenly weak. He put his head in his hands. Mike Greig who had picked up the file waited until Bruce raised his head.

"Can we proceed Mr Lewis? Would you like some water?" he asked already pouring from a jug into a glass which he moved before Bruce.

"I would like you to recall for me please what you were doing, where you were, and who can verify it say, from the 10th of this month to the 15th."

"I was at home. I took time off because my sister and her husband and their two children, spent two weeks with us. We did things with the children every day."

"Us?" Mike instantly queried.

"Yes, my my mother who has been living with my son Callum and me, ever since my wife left." the detective started to write in the folder. In the silence Bruce started to think, "Whereabouts did the accident take place," he asked.

"Near Pinners Hole.------ Do you know it?"

"Yes,"---He frowned. Bruce knew it as a long twisting lonely road across desolate marshland, quite close to home.

"Was she taking a short-cut to the hospital?" he asked, "because, to be frank with you, I don't know where she has been living, since she left me." He frowned and then corrected himself, "where she was living."

"You didn't know where she lived?" Mike's eyes bored through him.

"No.--Lindsay had left with her-- lover, Graham MacKendrick, the father of her baby. I have the letter she wrote me, and my mother saw them go together."

"Do you have or own any other vehicles, either at your farm or elsewhere, other than the Land Rover my officer saw this-morning?"

"Yes, I have a tractor and a lorry horse-box and a four-wheel farm bike and my car. Look, you dont think I've anything to do with this?" Bruce said, suddenly horrified at the implication. Mike leaned back in his chair, put the tips of his fingers together and silently regarded him. If you think you're going to make me squirm, then you've got another think coming, Bruce thought, as he met Mike's eyes unflinchingly.

"We have to ask questions, Sir. You say that your wife was living with a Mr. Graham MacKendrick?"

"Yes, that's what she told me. I asked her if she was happy and if he treated her well?---and she said, yes."

"Why should you have asked that, Mr. Lewis, when she left you for him?"

"Because, she had told my mother that he had threatened to leave her if she didn't have an abortion but it was too late for that to happen. And he appeared to have gone back to his wife."

"When did you last see your wife to ask those questions?"

"Only three weeks ago when she called to see our son, and she took him to see where he was going to live with her--------- but Callum couldn't tell us where it was."

"Do you have a lady-friend, Mr Lewis?"

Bruce frowned, the question took him aback. It was an affront. "No. Of course I don't," he said indignantly. Mike looked at his papers, "A--- Miss Fiona Brown?" The blood rushed to Bruce's face, "She is the young daughter of a friend of mine. She is at University. I think I ought to have my solicitor here, if you are implying misconduct on my part." Mike studied him, and thought, I've really have got him rattled now.

"By the way," Mike said, "Hospital records have you down as the father."

"But, she wanted the divorce because she told me that it was not my baby, but Graham's."

"Where did this man Graham MacKendrick live before he was supposed to be living with your wife?"

"At MacKendricks Garden Nursery, up the glen, close to where I live. His wife was my wife's best friend," he smiled a wry, bitter smile as he said it.

"I see, thank you," Mike scribbled on a pad. "Keep yourself available please, that will be all for now Mr Lewis." Mike said dismissing him.

"May I know where my wife was living?"

"On an estate, just outside Aberdeen." Mike said obliquely, sitting back watching him. Bruce shook his head in perplexity.

"It wasn't just the divorce was it, Mr. Lewis?" Mike said leaning forward,

"You were fighting her for sole custody of your son, Callum I believe?."

"Yes, I was." Bruce admitted, "but you can't think------"

"That is a motive Mr Lewis, that we have to examine." He shuffled the papers back into the file, gave it a smart tap on the desk and stood up,

"I will arrange for a car to take you home and my officer will examine all your vehicles. Please make them available to him" Bruce nodded. The interview was at an end--- for now. Bruce walked out, unseeing, unbelieving, that this could be happening to him. He sat in a daze in the back of the police car driving him home. His marriage had been over and yes, his love for Lindsay, his wife of twelve years had diminished as he had fought her for Callum to stay with him but, nevertheless for Lindsay's life to have been expunged in such dire and suspicious circumstances shocked him to the core of his being.

Back home, he took the police officer to the open-ended barn where he kept the horse-box, farm-bike, tractor and his BMW. His Land Rover was still parked at the front of the house. "Which garages do you have your vehicles serviced or repaired, Sir?"

"At Forfar Motors or the Tractor Tyre place." Bruce had nothing to hide and left him to it. He walked into the house where Vicky was waiting anxiously for his return. He told her briefly what had happened and that he was apparently a suspect as they were now examining all the other vehicles

She put her hands to her face, "Oh, no!" she said, equally shocked.

After a hurried phone call when the police car had gone, he drove to his solicitor to relate what had taken place and to seek his advice. Peter Duncan had been going fishing on his afternoon off when Bruce had rung him, but hadn't the heart to make him wait for another appointment. Bruce duly arrived in a lather of shock, indignation and helplessness. Peter in all his years as a solicitor had heard it all before, as his father had before him. He sat Bruce down, gave him a small dram of his best Laphroaig Whisky to calm him down.

"Now look Bruce, I have all of your movements, the times you consulted me and when we went to court, it is all on record, and then the crucial time you spent with the family over the last two weeks, that can also be easily corroborated."

"But it was the inference that I was fighting Lindsay for sole custody, the implication that it was a motive for killing her," Bruce ran his fingers through his hair in distraught helplessness. "My God, what are people going to think?"

"If you are summoned again for questioning I will accompany you, so don't worry. They have to go through a process of elimination before they can say that it was an accident by a hit and run driver. Callous though it is, these things happen. It is the coincidence of circumstances that is unfortunate in this case for you. You have to stand firm. Tell the truth,----- and don't worry my boy," the older man said kindly. "Is there anything else you need to tell me about?" Bruce thought, there was something worrying him,

"He asked if I had a lady-friend and of course I said, no. I haven't. Then he asked me about the daughter of a friend of mine---a Miss Fiona Brown." Peter frowned, his eyes narrowed. "Do you mean John Brown, the Naturalist, Professor Brown's daughter?" Bruce nodded, "Yes, they have been so kind to me and my family, that I can't bear to think that she could possibly be dragged into this."

"No,---- indeed." Peter murmured.

"There is absolutely nothing going on between us." Bruce reiterated.

"Well, there is nothing to worry about then, is there?"

"I suppose not, but why should he pick on her?" Bruce worried. Why indeed? Peter thought and felt a certain unease for the first time. She was certainly a wild one, that daughter of Brown.

"Do I arrange a funeral or should it be Graham MacKendrick?------The police appeared not to know where he was."

"Well, although she left you, you are not actually legally divorced yet, are you? So, I think the funeral will be your responsibility."

"Yes, I suppose so." Bruce said bleakly, thinking about Callum.

"You will have to wait for the police to clear this with you, so that might not happen for awhile" Peter warned.

*　　*　　*

When Bruce had left to go to see his solicitor, Vicky decided to phone John and tell him about Lindsay's shocking death. As soon as he answered she launched into the visit from the police and the fact that Bruce was taken for questioning as though he had deliberately murdered her. She paused---

"Yes, they've been here too." John said in clipped tones. "God knows why? I suppose it's because we know you."

"I hope you put in a good word for Bruce." she said and then went on anxiously, "I was ringing you to warn you that Bruce was questioned about Fiona."

"Why on earth should you be warning me?--- What could she possibly have to do with this sordid affair?" His voice was so cold, It was like a slap in the face to Vicky and flustered she dropped the phone. She picked it up,

"Hello, John---?" but he had put his phone down. She replaced the receiver slowly. What did it mean? This was a John she did not recognize. Her heart started to beat. She felt that she couldn't breathe, as though she had been punched in her stomach. In that moment something had been lost. She would not contact him again. She sat down in the silence that surrounded her and thought incongruously, we could have been going to be married!

She thought back to their last conversation about Bruce and Fiona and how she had challenged him about herself as to whether he had vetted her past as a suitable marriage partner? All she could think, was that he appeared to be frightened of any scandal that could touch him or his daughter. Although she had felt uneasy by what he had said, because she loved him, she had excused it as a father's anxiety about his daughter. Of course he wanted the girl to meet and marry a suitable man. Who wouldn't? but why was he so worried about her being a little fond of Bruce? It was only friendship after all. Unless that friendship implied a conspiracy of guilt. Ridiculous! Vicky thought. They were both upright good people.

Later, Vicky rang Jane's mobile to see where they were. They had decided to break the journey and had put up at a hotel for the night and were just going down for something to eat. "Please don't over-react in front of Callum dear, when I tell you that we have all had a terrible shock. Lindsay was found dead in her car which had been forced off the road, by another vehicle. She wasn't found for days because it had lain buried in a deep culvert and the poor girl had drowned. Bruce has been questioned by the police.

"Oh, really," Jane said in a controlled, neutral voice, for the benefit of Callum. "We are all okay. I'll phone you when we get back to-morrow mum. Lots of love from us all. Bye."

Vicky was dismayed two mornings later, to see the headline in the weekly paper, 'WELL KNOWN PUBLISHER QUESTIONED BY POLICE OVER ESTRANGED WIFE's DEATH.' If she hadn't already realized it, this would undoubtedly spell the death of her relationship with John. It was abhorrent to her, and by association must be doubly so to him, if he thought that his family were going to be dragged through the mire. She had a sudden picture of all his ancestors averting their eyes as they looked down on him from the walls as he climbed the staircase.

When Bruce saw the headlines, he paled. His business was already in dire financial straits. What on earth would this notoriety do for it, he thought? The phone rang, it was the police. "Sorry about this, sir, would you come in to give a DNA sample. We forgot to do it the other day. It will only take a moment." Bruce left the house grim-faced to drive to Aberdeen.

*   *   *

Permission was finally granted by the Procurator Fiscal for the funeral to take place. It was an ordeal to be got through. To match their feelings it was a drear day with lowering skies. The leaves were already falling, gusts of wind driving them across the windscreen and into swirling heaps of dark, wet russet. The fields were losing their greenness to an acid dank yellow. Vicky shuddered involuntarily and thought that it would only be her and Bruce and Lindsay's mother attending the funeral. Three people to remember, not many for a life, she thought, but was surprised to see as they entered the kirk that Beth, Ivor and Andrew Gilchrist were there, as well as Jean Ferguson. Next to her sat Morag but no Graham. She felt the pain of Mrs Cameron, Lindsay's mother, who had known nothing of her daughter leaving Bruce and Callum because of her pregnancy and affair with Graham. As for Beth, Vicky couldn't help thinking a little unkindly how she must be gloating over so much scandal and gossip to pass on. Perhaps she was being unjust to the woman she thought guiltily. Whereas, it was nice for Jean to come and show her sympathy and especially Morag, the wronged wife, for her to be here to remember happier times, when she and Lindsay had once been friends.

Bruce had stipulated with the minister that he didn't want any hymns. He too had presumed there would only be the three of them and none of them would feel like singing. They recited psalm 23, the Lord's Prayer and listened to the readings and the minister's sympathetic address followed by the burial. Afterwards, Ivor came and spoke a brief word of sympathy to Bruce, there was a pat on the back from an embarrassed Andrew, their son. Jean expressed her sympathy to him Morag met his eyes across the pews and acknowledged him with a nod before she quickly disappeared. Beth waylaid Vicky and oozed compassion and indignation over their plight. And then it was over.

Vicky and Bruce drove back in silence. Bruce was feeling sorry for Morag, he would have liked to have asked her about Graham. Was he around, had he gone back to her, or had he vanished? It suddenly occurred to him that she too could be thought of as 'having a motive'. and he wondered whether she had come under police scrutiny as he had.

His mother had told him about her phone call to John. He wouldn't have expected him to come to the funeral of someone he had never met but he was dismayed at his reaction to his mother's phone call. He had agreed to publish John's book when he had finished it, and possibly another book about his experience with the release of of wolves, when he returned from America, but it now looked as though John wanted no more to do with any of them.

Bruce had phoned John several times but neither he nor Fiona had answered the phone. He began to feel that maybe he shouldn't get in touch with her in case his phone was being tapped and it would be misconstrued. She had been such a supportive pal to him through his troubles. Her continuing friendship was important to him but not at the cost of any scandal to her. Vicky seemed to have been on the same wavelength as his thoughts when she suddenly asked him about Fiona. "Do you know when she's due back in London?"

"About the beginning of October, I think. She may have gone earlier so that she can see Callum at Jane and Mark's. before she starts Uni. I have phoned but nobody answers, so perhaps John has gone to America by now." Vicky digested this silently. "I wonder what she will do for Christmas?"

"She'll come home, she told me she wanted to go hunting. She won't be alone with James and Marian there."

"We could invite her to spend Christmas day with us."

"Yes, but only if this ghastly business of Lindsay's accident is cleared up. I wouldn't want her implicated in any way. She is a friend."

"I think she is a bit more than a friend, I think she is in in love with you." Vicky said, rather daringly. "She only has eyes for you. Haven't you noticed?" He looked at her amazed. "Don't be ridiculous, mother. I'm twelve years older than her." but he thought, someone else must have told the police, for them to have asked him if she was his lady-friend. If she loved him as his mother had appeared to notice, then other people must have noticed it too. It shook him rather. He had come to rely on her, but he thought that was because she loved Callum. He drove thoughtfully down the drive. Once indoors he set about lighting the woodburner and getting some warmth into the place. He also felt that he didn't want to share with his mother what exactly he did feel about Fiona.

Jane rang Bruce most evenings so that Callum could speak to his father. London had been a big adventure and revelation to Callum as he told Bruce about going to the Tower of London, Madam Tussauds, the Natural History Museum, picnics in Epping Forest. Tonight, he was telling his father that he had even been to see Henry and William's posh school, on an introductory pre-term day. "They thought I was a new pupil, dad, and they asked if I had any Latin or Greek" he laughed delightedly. "I said, What? We all went to see Aunty Jane take a ballet class-- for boys," he said incredulously--" and Fiona came too. She wants to take ballet classes."

"How often do you see Fiona?" Bruce asked him,

"She's staying with us until her friends come back to the house they share." He said importantly. "I've been there."

"I see," said Bruce, "Is she there with you now?"

"Fiona-a--," Bruce heard him call, daddy wants to talk to you."

"Bruce? Hello."

"Fiona, what a surprise. I didn't know you had gone."

"I know,---- daddy rushed me back here.---I'm sorry about your wife—her accident------How are things back home?"

"Pretty awful at the moment. You are well out of it. Hit-and-run driver and they suspect me! It's plastered all over the papers. Callum doesn't know, anything yet." he warned. "We've had the funeral. Your father hasn't been in touch with us at all. Has he gone to America?"

"No, the release of the wolves won't take place until the spring, to give them more chance to establish themselves before a winter. He's here in London. He's always busy, seeing colleagues, planning lectures, I don't even see him. He stays at his club." she explained.

"I don't suppose we will see you until Christmas, then."

"That's right," she said." At half- term, I shall probably stay here to revise. Callum will soon be coming back for his new term, won't he?"

"Uh-huh."

"Will he be going back on the train on his own?" she asked. "Maybe I could bring him back" she said impulsively, "just for the weekend."

"Bruce smiled," We'll see," he said non-committedly. "Take care Fiona."

"And you, It will all work out, Bruce, don't worry,-- love you,." she said lightly, before putting the phone down.

"Mmm. Love you too," he murmured to himself, then shook his head

Fiona remained thoughtful as she put the phone down after speaking to Bruce. She was resentful that her father had insisted on taking her back to London way before her term had started. He obviously hadn't really believed her, although he said he had at the time, when he had summoned her to his office and demanded to know if she was involved in the death of Bruce's wife? She had stared at him in amazement until he had broken down and told her that she was all he had. He was so afraid that she might have acted impulsively, on the spur of the moment out of her love for Bruce.

"And what do you believe that I am likely to have done, daddy?" she had asked coldly. "How did I kill her? Have you looked at my car? Didn't you show them all to the police? That's what they came to see, wasn't it? Didn't they see my car, and yours and all our vehicles?"

"Yes, they did." he had replied quietly.--------"but I saw you the very next day talking with Morag MacKendrick in our yard.. Was that wise? What were you even doing with her? Why had she driven here, to our place?" Fiona had felt her face redden under his grilling.

"She rang me to ask if I could let her have a few bales of hay. She was running short. I had got plenty, so I let her have a few bales. She drove her Land Rover round to the barns for them. That's all. I was just helping her out."

"Swear to me, Fiona, that you had nothing to do with the accident."

"Of course I didn't. How could you think that I could?" His eyes bored into hers as they stared unflinchingly at each other for an interminable time before he dropped his eyes and muttered, "No, no, of course not. I had to ask. I'm sorry, but apparently a Land Rover was seen that morning on the road near to where the accident happened." She had shrugged her shoulders and repeated that she had nothing to do with the accident as she looked into the gravity of her father's eyes. And then he had said almost wearily, that he had this important meeting to attend at the Natural History Museum and that he could take her to London ready to start her new term even if it was a little early. She was to pack her bags that evening. She would have the time to buy her books and do a little research before her term started. He had been quite implacable about taking her back. She had been startled at the thought, that he was frightened for her, or that he didn't believe her and thought that she was capable of such a malicious act. Her own father! Her face became impassive, she felt emotionless and ice-cold.

*   *   *

When Vicky came in from stabling the horses for the night. Bruce told her, "I've just spoken to Callum. He's happy. Fiona is staying with them.

Has Jane told you?" he asked.

"No, perhaps she's just gone for the day or week-end."

"I spoke to her, asked about her father. She said he was staying at his club in London and seeing colleagues and lecturing, He isn't going to America until after Christmas."

"Oh, do you think she knew what was going on here?" Vicky asked.

"Yes, I think so. Her father had taken her to London way before she needed to go, to protect her, I suppose, from any unwarranted police intrusion by association with us, I guess."

"Mmm?" Vicky felt it still did not excuse John's behaviour to her.

"Fiona was as sympathetic as she could be, with Callum there." he said. He yawned and stretched, "This whole business has knocked me for six, I'm going to try and catch up with all my paperwork, before dinner." Vicky retired into the kitchen to prepare their evening meal. When she came in to lay the table she found Bruce with his head in his hands and the table still strewn with folders and papers. He looked up at her, he looked ghastly,

"Whatever is the matter?" she asked him.

"Apparently, Lindsay has emptied our account. It has been closed. I had transferred some money into it, for the financial settlement and a loan to bolster my business up, and now, it has all gone," he said ashen-faced. I found a letter from the bank warning me ages ago, but I hadn't opened it, with everything going on. I was going to take out a mortgage on the steading. I'm facing bankruptcy, mother." The dinner grew cold in the oven, neither of them could eat.

"But, what has she done with the money?" Vicky asked. "You are her husband. Surely you have a right to it? Go and get Peter Duncan's advice tomorrow," she advised.

"Have you any idea how much I owe that man already, and the courts?" Then another thought struck him. "They will say that this was yet another motive to kill her." Vicky shook her head. "It doesn't matter, you have to get legal advice." They both spent a sleepless night, tossing and turning. When dawn broke it was a relief to get up. Bruce swallowed cups of black coffee for breakfast and waited impatiently for a decent time to ring Peter. When he finally left the house, Vicky rang Jane's mobile and told her what had happened.

"Oh, my goodness, what a terrible situation" Jane said, "What can we do to help? Callum is really fine here. I know his school term starts soon, but if it is better that he stays on with us, we can get him a term in Henry's year at their school. They are not due to go back until the end of the month. Talk it over with Bruce and let us know. By the way, John left Fiona all alone in the house she shares with other students when it is term, which is weeks away, so she has been staying here on and off with us. She has made herself useful looking after the boys when I have to teach. I don't know whether John knows where his daughter is. Still, as you know she is a very capable girl. She knows her way around London. Speak to you later, mum, Bye."

Bruce came in and slumped in a chair. "Well, Peter has told me that the police hold the key to Lindsay's flat and we can do nothing until a verdict is brought in about her death. So it's a waiting game mum, while the house and business crashes about my ears." He pulled a face, "I'd better go up to Edinburgh as soon as possible, if you can cope here mum?"

"Of course. You must. I shall be alright." She told him what Jane had suggested.

"Oh, I don't know. Is it selfish of me, when I say that I miss my boy?"

"No, of course it isn't, I'll make plans to go and get him."

*   *   *

CHAPTER THIRTEEN

Vicky rang her daughter Jane, then booked her flight to London. She packed lightly, she was only going to stay one night with Jane before flying back with Callum. She arranged with Andrew Gilchrist to look in on the horses and check that they were alright, because of Bruce being away in Edinburgh. They would be back the next day, she promised.

The flight took all the hassle out of driving all that way.

It gave her time to consider Bruce and his predicament but inevitably she found herself day-dreaming about John and the time they had first met again in London, how happy she had been with their growing friendship and how it had all seemed to fall apart in an instant. She had been such an old fool, she thought. Well, it would never happen again. Once bitten, twice shy. She smiled wryly, the truth was, she was bitterly hurt by his silence.

Once she had landed she took a taxi into the centre of London to Sotheby's, She tucked herself into the familiar little old lift and didn't forget to turn herself around when the lift door opened. Madison Haynes rose to greet her. This time there was no-one else with her. She gave her the ring together with the letter from the Factor which she hoped would give the ring its legitimate provenance. Madison Haynes disappeared with it for quite a while. When she returned she said that subject to authentication, which could take some time, they would then prepare the papers for auction. They would keep her informed. Vicky gave her

Jane's telephone number and address for this. Her daughter would attend the auction on her behalf, she informed her. She was given a receipt and the ring was gone!

As Vicky carefully tucked the receipt away she had a horrible feeling that she was betraying something of Scotland's heritage, as John had said when he thought she might sell it. She had the feeling that he would be dismayed at her action. God knows where it would end up, she thought. She was doing it to rescue her son, although he too was oblivious of what she was doing. Her mouth felt dry. She couldn't swallow. She even felt a little faint. Well she had done it now. She was glad to sit down in the small restaurant there, and ordered herself coffee, some smoked salmon and scrambled egg. As she looked around her seeing people in close conversation together, she wished that things were different between her and John and that he was here sitting with her.

She decided to take the underground to Woodford and a taxi from there to Jane's at Woodford Green. It had been quite a day. Now she could relax with Jane. The house was quiet, All the boys were out with Fiona. They had gone to the zoo Jane said, and would be back shortly. Vicky gave Jane the receipt and told her that Sotheby's would get in touch with her.

"I hope you don't mind doing this for me dear, but it was the only way that I could help Bruce out of his trouble."

"No, of course not. I only hope that it's as valuable as you seem to think it is. What do I do if it doesn't make its proposed valuation price? Do I withdraw it?"

"Well, yes, if its only hundreds instead of thousands, but they will write to you and give you a valuation to consider before they enter it for auction. Just let me know, okay?"

"Okay. Have there been any developments from the police yet?"

"No, I suppose it takes a long time to visit all the garages to examine cars, and considering all the wild and hidden places around us, it would seem to be an impossible job, Vicky said.

"Well, except that they would be looking for someone with a motive and then look at their connections etc. which would narrow it down."

"I suppose so, but then if they don't find anything, it could just be an accident and whoever was responsible was too afraid and cowardly to report it." There was a knock at the door,

"That will be Fiona and the boys."

"Let me go," said Vicky getting up.

"Grandma!" the boys chorused in surprise when she opened the door. Fiona ushered the boys in. Over tea, Vicky heard all about their day at the zoo. When she told Callum that she had come to take him back for his new term, Fiona said,

"Oh, Vicky I could have brought Callum back for you. We were going to go back on the train weren't we," she said looking at him with obvious disappointment.

"I had some business to do in London," Vicky explained.

"Oh, Callum, aren't you going to come to school with us, after all." Henry said pleadingly. "Oh go on, stay here with us." both boys chorused.

"Popular boy," Jane said with a smile.

"Daddy is missing you, and Tweed." She turned to Jane.

"Perhaps you could all fly up to us for Christmas?" Vicky invited.

"That would be super," Fiona said. "I'll get a pony for Henry and William." The boys shouted, "Yes please."

"Thank you, we'll see." Jane said. "Meanwhile young man, we had better go upstairs and get you packed up for to-morrow. Uncle Mark and I and the boys will drive you both to the airport." When they were alone Vicky asked Fiona, "How is your father?"

"He's alright, he rings me most evenings. I haven't seen much of him. He had to come to London so he brought me down with him, if a little early for my term," she explained.

"I see, I wondered where you had both disappeared to."

Oh, Vicky, I'm so sorry. When the police came asking us questions about the accident that Lindsay had and our association with Bruce, I think it frightened him."

"Why should it have frightened him?" Fiona looked away and frowned, "I think he thought that I was too fond of Bruce and would get myself mixed up with what is going on now---the police---and everything."

"I see,--- and are you fond of Bruce.?"

"Oh, there's absolutely nothing between us," she went on hurriedly,

"But yes, I think he is a lovely man, a good friend," she said looking Vicky squarely in the eye, as much as to say, so there!---- ---She paused,

"I feel awful that dad has not spoken to you,----" Vicky made no comment.

"How is Bruce?" Fiona asked.

"In dire trouble financially. Lindsay drained their joint bank account."

"Bitch !" the word exploded from Fiona, taking Vicky aback. She went on pretending not to have heard her, thinking that this was how the young spoke today. "We haven't heard any more from the police, but the Procurator Fiscal released the body for burial. It just remains for me to tell Callum." Fiona hung on her words and nodded. "Oh, poor Bruce, what will he do?"

Vicky shook her head, "I don't know."

Fiona left early the next morning leaving a little card for Callum to open when he was on the plane. His uncle and aunt, Henry and William waved them off at the airport. "Until Christmas---," they shouted.

Callum was excited to be flying home and couldn't understand why his grandma had to hold his hand as they took off. There was nothing at all to be scared of, as they soared over a populated urban sprawl which gave way to fields and rivers, and then they were up high above the clouds. He turned to open the envelope that Fiona had left for him. He took the card out, and studied the picture. It was of a cream Highland pony, on purple heathered moorland with a mountain in the distance. He smiled. It reminded him of Tweed, "Look," he said to Vicky. She admired it. He opened the card. She had written, 'Looking forward to Christmas when we will ride together. Fiona.' He put it away in his pocket.

Vicky agonized whether it was right to tell him about his mother or should she leave it for Bruce to tell him. It would depend if he was home yet. She decided to leave it unless he actually asked about his mother. In no time at all they were landing, out through the airport and picking her car up for the few miles back home. They stopped on the way for something to eat and to buy some essentials. Once home, after dumping his case Callum ran to the stables to see Tweed and Jet.

Bruce came home for the week-end. There was a mountain of post for him to attend to, but not before he had lifted Callum up to him and kissed and hugged his little boy. He listened to all his excited recounting of his adventures in London with his cousins and Fiona.

"What would I do without you man," he said looking at him with tears in his eyes. Callum looked wonderingly at him, and frowning a little, he asked,

"What's the matter, daddy?" Bruce grasped the nettle and said,

"Sometime while you were away, your mummy died in a car accident."

"Mummy's dead?" Bruce nodded. Callum knew what dead meant. He had seen dead lambs and a badger and foxes that had lain dead on the road because a car had hit them. Suddenly a thought struck him.

"Fiona's mummy is dead. My mummy is dead.-----That makes us the same."

"Well,--- yes." Bruce said a little uncertainly. Callum got off his lap and ran to the stables to tell Tweed. Bruce sat staring after him. He wasn't at all sure quite how affected Callum was by the news of his mother. It had been a long time since he had seen her. except for her brief visit when she took him out just before her death. The fact that his grandma had been a surrogate mother for him all these months had cushioned the blow for him. Wearily he turned to opening his post.

The police had sent him a copy of his DNA findings. He was not the father of Lindsay's baby. "I knew that," he muttered under his breath. A score of bills followed, He put them on one side. Quite how he was going to pay them, he didn't know. He put them in order of urgency. The next letter was a summons to attend the Procurator Fiscal's Court for a hearing and verdict. Thank God, he thought, it's about time. We need to move on. He felt that he had been imprisoned in a time warp of dastardly suspicion, which made him feel as though he was guilty. It was a horrible situation. Vicky came in and wanted to know how Callum had taken the news.

"I'm not really sure. He seemed to have accepted it with little emotion. He's gone to tell Tweed." Vicky nodded wisely, "He'll be alright."

Before he went back to school Vicky took Callum shopping for new school clothes. He had had a sudden spurt of growth and pleaded for long grown-up, grey flannel trousers which she bought for him plus two new royal-blue pullovers, some shirts and a new school tie because he had lost the old one. They made a day of it having lunch in a nice restaurant. It was her treat. At some point in their conversation, he said to her, "Fiona and I are the same now." "Oh, In what way?" Vicky asked?"

"Her mother is dead too, that makes us the same," he said firmly.

"Just as though that gave him comfort," she told Bruce later.

*   *   *

CHAPTER FOURTEEN

If the weather wasn't too bad Vicky would ride Jet and lead
Tweed on a halter most days. At weekends she and Callum
would ride out together. Because it was autumn, and not
wishing to churn-up grassland, they rode along quiet lanes,
walking and trotting, which was a good way to get the
horses into shape after an idle summer. Because she had
known that John was in London she had taken to riding
along a narrow unused lane that ran through the middle
of his estate cutting it in two. This gave her a good circular
ride. She was pretty sure that James knew that she was riding
the lane. She had seen him wave to her in the distance and
she hoped that if John knew, he would not mind her taking
this liberty.

A large open-ended barn stood at the side of the lane.
In the summer it had lain empty and the wind used to
gust through it banging the corrugated sides and roof and
terrifying Jet with its thunderous claps. She was pleased
to see that one half of it now had been filled to the roof
with new hay and the other half was part filled with what
looked like, to Vicky, bales of old musty looking straw and
hay. There was room for a fork-lift to drive in-between She
supposed that this was where John had told her that Fiona
had worked for two days on her own, getting her stock of
feed and bedding in for her horses, when they came back
from livery for Christmas. Frankly, she would never hang
on to old hay and straw. Vicky could only guess that up here

you never threw old hay or straw out because the summers were too unpredictable and every bit of hay and straw was precious.

Callum told her that he thought that it would be great to operate the fork-lift but Fiona wouldn't let him. "I should think not," she said as they rode past and looked up at the immense height of the barn. "If those fell on you, you would be buried for ever." She instantly wished that she hadn't said that, but Callum laughed out loud, thankfully unperturbed.

*   *   *

Bruce sat with Peter Duncan beside him in court. Morag and Graham Mackendrick sat a distance apart from one another. Detective Mike Greig sat unsmiling, impartial, holding his files. The Procurator Fiscal summed up,

"The suspicious circumstances in which this poor unfortunate woman and her unborn child met their death has needed a criminal investigation. There was a tangled web of relationships with a divorce pending." He stopped and looked over his glasses at them, before adjusting them back again and proceeding.

"However,--- the offending vehicle has not yet been found, Deliberate or not, it was a callous and criminal act to leave this woman and her unborn child to die." Once again the glasses came off and were swung around in his hand, while he fixed each one of them with a penetrating stare. The glasses went back on "The police have certain evidence of make and paintwork which is on record," and he looked across at Mike Greig, who nodded in confirmation.

"So,---at this time, I can only give an open verdict of unlawful death, by a person or persons unknown. Therefore this case remains adjourned for further investigation." They stood up as the Procurator Fiscal walked out. Bruce had kept an eye on Graham and waylaid him before he had a chance to disappear. Graham looked scared. "I want to know," Bruce asked, "were you living with Lindsay at her flat in Aberdeen?"

"No," he mumbled, his face full of guilt. "She gave me the money to buy a flat for her. We had quarreled. It was over between us, and I--- left her and went back to Morag." he ended sheepishly, "but I had nothing to do with the accident." he added quickly.

"No? Even if she would have taken you for every penny you had got, for the child, your child.----- You have ruined our lives." Bruce shouted back angrily as Graham hurried out of the courtroom. Peter Duncan restrained Bruce from following him. Mike Greig had been watching with interest the interplay between the two men.

*   *   *

"Well, it's neither one thing nor the other, Bruce told Vicky, once he was home as he recounted the verdict. We are all still guilty until proven innocent."

"Don't you mean it the other way round dear, innocent until proved guilty"

"I suppose so, but it doesn't feel like that," Bruce said with feeling. "By the way, I've been given the key to Lindsay's flat and I would appreciate it if you would come with me and help me empty it."

*   *   *

Jane was stylishly dressed in a smart black suit for the occasion as she walked into the auction room at Sotheby's.

She carried a file under her arm, took a seat, opened the file and read the write-up on the provenance of the Victorian ring bearing the crest of the House of Saxe-Coburg and Gotha. 'Well, she wouldn't have thought that that necessarily gave it provenance that it had belonged to the Queen or to HRH Prince Albert, it could have belonged to one of his relatives. She read on,' However, there was the Factor's letter from the shooting lodge, which lent credence that it might well be.. She wondered whether anyone would take that chance. She watched as she saw various pieces of jewellery being bought for sums of money that made her gasp and then it was the turn of the ring.

Jane felt a nervousness that she hadn't encountered for a long time since she had danced with the company at Covent Garden. The auctioneer described it. "This beautifully made gold Victorian ring with the prestigious crest of the House of Saxe-Coburg, together with the letter A scrolled beneath the crest engraved on a bloodstone, which might appertain to HRH Pince Albert. This ring was found in a loch adjoining the Balmoral estate and the Factor's letter noting Queen Victoria's visit to this particular location with John Brown, where it was recorded that Queen Victoria had said that she had lost a ring" The auctioneer looked up pausing for breath,

"Now, ladies and gentlemen who is going to start us off with the bidding? Five thousand is the starting price,? Here, thank you," he indicated someone seated up front. It was quickly followed by mounting tens of thousands from all over the room. There were people bidding by proxy, on the phone and by internet. The auctioneer waiting for the persons to be instructed on how to bid.

Jane felt that there was something about an auction that sent people into a frenzied mode of out-doing the next person which, in her cautious way made her feel that it could be highly dangerous. Like some high adrenaline drug, it would soon become out of control. The bids came fast and furious, from all quarters. When it reached a quarter of a million Jane thought she might faint, What a pity her mother wasn't here to see her ring vindicated from the sneering doubts she had cast on it. Never in her life had she been so surprised. She had half thought that it wouldn't make its reserve price and the shame of it would make her slink out of Sotheby's never to darken its doors again. Now, the bids were slowing down somewhat. It seemed to be between someone on the floor and someone being instructed on the phone. The phone got it. Three hundred and fifty thousand pounds? Once?---Twice?---going-- the gavel came down. Sold, to the client on the phone. It was over. The frustrating thing was that she couldn't tell her mother who had bought it !

She made her way to the office and made the financial transaction minus Sotheby's percentage, into the bank. A celebratory luncheon had been put on for the sellers and buyers, but Jane declined as she was on her own. If only Mark had been with her, she could really have enjoyed the whole experience. Instead she flipped open her mobile and called her mother.

"What? No!" Vicky exclaimed. I don't believe it.

*   *   *

As Bruce and Vicky drove out of the glen to go to Lindsay's flat in Aberdeen, they couldn't help glancing across at Graham and Morag's place. Two police cars were parked outside.

"They are getting the third degree now," Bruce remarked grimly, as they drove past. Once out of the glen it was a fast road to Aberdeen. The flat was on a modern estate with lots of look-alike roads which would have taken quite a bit of finding without his sat-nav. The key was shiny and new as he put it into the lock, and he couldn't help but think of Lindsay handling the key that now lay in his hands. When they got inside, the place was typically Lindsay, untidy with baskets of her washing, parcels spilling open of newly purchased baby-clothes, bedding and nappies, newspapers and magazines strewn about.

It wasn't a bad-sized flat and it had all the basics in furnishings, but to think that Lindsay had given-up her country-style outdoor life for this pokiness dismayed Bruce. How she had felt when Graham had left her, he couldn't bear to imagine. No wonder she had been fighting him for Callum to go and live with her when she was stuck here all on her own. How he would have hated this. He recalled her bravado when they had last spoken, that she was happily living with Graham, she would fight him to the last penny for Callum. She wanted her horse sold and so on. He shook his head. Had she been so miserable with him that she chose this? Had she rented this flat? put a down payment on it? or bought it with their joint account that she had drained, or what? He needed to find her paperwork and started opening drawers.

Meanwhile, Vicky had brought up some cardboard boxes and started filling them with the baby items. Next, she gathered Lindsay's clothes out of the wardrobe and drawers, One lonely picture of her horse Jet, was hanging on the wall. She took it down and placed it on top of her clothes. She looked at Bruce to see what headway he was making.

"There is nothing here, mum, absolutely nothing. She must have had debit or credit cards, bank statement, rent-book or deeds, something."

"Perhaps the police took all that away with them."

"Well, they could have told me," he said frustrated and annoyed.

"The station is in the middle of Aberdeen, we'll call on them."

*   *   *

That evening, after dinner, Bruce emptied the contents of the large envelope that the police had given him after signing for it. Lindsay's credit and debit cards were there with their latest joint bank statement, showing the money she had taken for the flat and the purchase of a car, pram, cot, baby clothes and all the furnishing of the flat. It had come to a very substantial amount. With the remainder of his money she had opened an account solely in her name at another bank. Lindsay had been driving the car which was now a total write-off. Maybe he would be able to claim compensation for that, and if he sold the flat and furnishings, he could at least recoup some of his money, but that would all take time, he thought, and time was something he hadn't got. But it was the thinking and the planning behind the deception that really smote his heart. Oh, Lindsay, Lindsay, however did it come to this! He found forms that she had been trying to fill in, after the divorce would have gone through, claiming for benefits as a single parent mother.

*   *   *

As Bruce pored over his sums scribbled on endless pieces of A4, he said to Vicky. "This place has got to go on the market, and quickly if I am to save the business."

"Is it really as bad as that? Have you contacted the bank?"

"It's the weekend. No, I was waiting for them to contact me, I cannot pay the interest on my loan any longer, and I don't think they are going to let me extend it," he said as he reached for the phone. He listened after pressing all the required digits, frowned, shook his head and pressed a digit again for the message to be repeated. Slowly he replaced the phone, "I don't get it," he said. "They keep on saying that I have got three hundred and fifty thousand pounds in my account. I'm bloody dreaming!" he said. "It's a mistake." He picked the phone up again, pressing the digits carefully, he listened again, before replacing the phone, a look of total bewilderment and consternation on his face as he looked at Vicky. She smiled and said quietly,

"I sold the ring!"

"Oh, mum, you did that for me. I'm so sorry, but thank you very much. I cannot believe it was that valuable."

"John was able to get some provenance that it could have been a ring that Queen Victoria lost when she was on her travels around the highlands,"

CHAPTER FIFTEEN

It was mid-week and Vicky was riding her usual circular course on Jet, leading Tweed. It was a fine but cold day, the trees were all stripped of their leaves and covered in a sparkling hoar frost. It would soon be Christmas. Both horses were anxious to trot on along the lanes, until she slowed them to a walk along the lane intersecting John's estate, past the big hay barn. Suddenly the mare stopped abruptly before letting out a high-pitched whinny.

"What's the matter girl," Vicky said, urging her on. The mare refused to go, and was looking intently with pricked ears up the lane to where the figure of a man riding a big bay horse was gradually coming into view as they climbed an incline toward them. She heard the other horse whinny back. Vicky had never met anyone before on this particular ride and was curious to see who it was. The mare suddenly decided she wanted to know too, and stepped out eagerly. As they got closer the other rider lifted his hand in acknowledgement, and she suddenly realized with a beating heart, that it was John. They drew abreast, "Vicky. Good morning. How are you?"

"I didn't recognize you," she said. "I thought you were away in America. I hope you don't mind me riding here?"

"Why should I? The lane is public, and I wouldn't mind if it wasn't."

"Oh,--- I wasn't sure."

"Can we talk, Vicky?" He said urgently. She was thinking, the nerve of the man. As though nothing had happened.

"I don't think that there is any thing left to say, John. You've made it abundantly clear to me, by your long silence, that you wanted nothing more to do with me and my family." She went to move Jet forward and ride past him, but he turned the big bay and fell into step beside her.

"I know, it was disgraceful. I'm really sorry. Can you forgive me?" Vicky kept her eyes on the road, "No, I'm sorry John. I don't think I can. How can I ever trust you again?---what you have put me through,-------- no explanation, nothing from you for months?---- How could I ever begin to—understand?" She took a big breath. ------"You said that you loved me and wanted to marry me----but obviously you changed your mind------" Her throat constricted and she stopped.----- "It's too painful. It's over between you and me." She urged Jet into a trot to leave him, but he grabbed the reins and the mare swung round held by him. Tweed was suddenly jerked off his feet and became entangled and tried to kick the mare.

"How dare you, John! Let me go." He could see the predicament she was in with the two horses, and let go of Jet's bridle as he dismounted and untangled Tweed's lead rein.

"Vicky, we need to talk. Please come back to the house with me. I need to speak with you in private."

She had started to shake, both with the cold and emotion.

"Alright," she said, finally, "but it had better be good!" He mounted the bay and they trotted in silence to the house where they stabled the horses first, before he escorted Vicky into the warmth of the kitchen. She sat down while he busied himself making coffee for them. When he sat opposite her he was shocked to see how pale she had become and it tore at his heart. They both sat for a while embracing the heat from the mugs into their frozen hands and sipping the warmth into them until he could see a little colour coming back into her cheeks. He started to speak.

"Thank you for giving me this time.---- It is true. I have treated you despicably, even though I love you, dearly. You have to believe me on that." Vicky's head came up abruptly and she frowned. He went on hurriedly.

"I had a reason which I couldn't ---can't divulge—"he stopped. He was breathing hard with the difficulty of choosing his words carefully----"I er--I made you hate me quite deliberately," he looked up at her, with pain written all over his face. "It was the only thing I could do. Believe me, I hated doing it to you."

"But why? Are you going to tell me the reason?"

"No, I can't. That's the awful thing about it." Vicky sighed and stood up, "Oh well, John, nothing has changed. I don't understand a word you've said." She started to zip up her jacket.

"It's to do with Fiona," he blurted out quickly.

She waited.

"This is just between us?" he muttered anxiously.

She nodded. "Of course," and sat down. John took a deep breath before saying, "I thought that maybe she was already implicated in ---in Lindsay's accident." Vicky's eyebrows shot up questioningly as she looked at him. -----

"Whatever made you think that?" she said shocked. He shook his head and didn't answer, then----- "I questioned her. She swore to me that she wasn't and I believe her, but I suppose I panicked and thought it best if I took her away.

149

My daughter is everything to me and I feared for her and wanted to protect her."

"But what made you even think that about Fiona?" she persisted. He remained silent as though struggling with himself.------------ "I knew that she loved Bruce and I also know that she can be very impulsive. I was just frightened for her." He looked at her.---------- "I didn't know what to do about us." he said lamely.

"I knew you were worried about Fiona and her association with Bruce in case she could be implicated in this horrible thing," Vicky said, "although I can't believe you actually thought that she was capable of----of----" words failed her as she put her hand across her mouth. She took a big breath and started again "As her father you were trying to protect her by dropping us. You didn't want any breath of scandal to touch her. I can understand that, even if I think it was cowardly of you not to be more frank with me. The thing is, John, that nothing has changed or been resolved. This horrible accident. It is still hanging over all our heads. Fiona is, for the time being back at her University and therefore not in close communication with Bruce, but she is a woman in her own right now and I don't think that she will be dictated to by her father as to where her affections lie."

"No," he said quietly, she won't."

"So, where does all this leave us?" He looked at her,---- ------- "Can you forgive me?---------- Can we start again?" he pleaded.

"I don't honestly know. It has just made me very unsure of you. I'm sorry, I can't help it," she said. "Perhaps I need time. I do understand how much your daughter means to you, but my son means the same to me. You chose to be indifferent to my feelings in your misguided rush to protect her. Would you treat me like this again? --------and just drop me? I don't know."

He went over to her and cupped her face in his hands and searched her face. "I will never do it again. Please forgive me. I'm so sorry."

"Something has been damaged between us John," she said sadly.

"Yes, I know and I'm so sorry. I will never hurt you again." he said fervently looking at her.." Please forgive me darling Vicky? "he pleaded. "I have missed you so very much. I've thought about you every day, wondering what you were thinking—what you were doing? Why did you come to London without telling me? We could have met up." She stared at him in amazement. "Ditto." she threw back at him quickly, with a withering look.

"Okay, point taken. I'm sorry."

"I went to London to bring Callum back for his new term."

"Mm?"

"Yes, I was only there one night." She suddenly found that she could not look at him as she remembered that she had sold the ring, part of Scotland's heritage. Guilt flooded her. But there was no way he could know this. And there was no way she was going to tell him. She was suddenly appalled at her own deviousness. She heard him continue,

"One night only? how exhausting."

"Not really, I flew." All the time, she was thinking as she deliberated whether to tell him about the ring or not, until the moment passed and it was too late.

"What's been happening at home then, with Bruce?"

"We had the Procurator Fiscal's inquest. Death by unlawful killing by person or persons unknown. The case has been adjourned for further investigation. They allowed the funeral, and for her flat to be cleared. And Bruce found out that Lindsay had drained their joint account and left him in dire financial straits."

"How is he?"

"Just about bearing up, I think. At least he is assured of having Callum. That is a comfort to him."

"Yes, indeed." He paused, "and what about us? Do we have a future together?" She shook her head, "I don't know John."

"Alright, we'll take it slowly and I will try and rebuild your trust in me. We can start again as friends, can't we?" He searched her face anxiously. She smiled a sad little smile, before whispering, "We could try." He embraced her gently, and kissed her hair.

"Will you come to America with me and be my she-wolf mate? She smiled in spite of herself. "I thought we were going to go slowly with our friendship. You are pushing me John. How can I say anything at this moment, when only an hour ago I thought it was all over between us. I was never going to speak to you ever again. I will tell you, one way or the other, but I thought that I had made up my mind once and now I need time to think about it. Please let's take things slowly. Let's hope that this wretched case will soon be resolved."

"Alright, my darling. I'm sorry. I don't blame you. A little time you shall have. Come on, let's get the horses and I will ride back with you."

Alone afterwards, as she pondered on their conversation. She wondered, was he still holding back on telling her everything, the real truth as to why he suspected his daughter's involvement with Lindsay's death. He had said that he knew she loved Bruce. Well, they all knew that. Perhaps he thought she was capable of some misguided action and had feared for her---- Even as she thought it, she knew that he had not given her sufficient reason for his actions and that she mistrusted him still. She would not tell Jane about this. She was always so perceptive about people and yet she had forged a strong friendship with Fiona. Perhaps it was because they were both strong decisive characters. She thought about Bruce, on whom the burden of suspicion rested. If she had to protect him against her relationship with John and Fiona, then she would.

*   *   *

CHAPTER SIXTEEN

It was Christmas eve, snow hung on the mountains giving the landscape a traditional festive air. At 'the Croft', the flames licked and leapt around the logs in the wood-burner, throwing out its warmth and cosiness and making the Christmas tree exude its pungent aromatic pine fragrance throughout the room. Fiona, who had come home from Uni. a few days ago by train, was helping Callum to decorate the tree, Vicky was making mince pies in the kitchen and Bruce had gone to the airport to pick up Jane, Mark and their boys, Henry and William, who were coming to stay for Christmas.

Fiona and Callum only just had time to lay the wrapped-up presents around the tree, before they heard the sound of Bruce returning. Vicky went to the door to welcome them and they all trooped in stamping their feet and rubbing their hands, shedding their coats and greeting one another with hugs and kisses. Jane sank into a settee in front of the fire, kicked off her shoes and stretched her stockinged feet toward the warmth. Fiona flopped beside her asking how the flight had been. Mark and Bruce carried the cases upstairs whilst the boys admired the tree and eyed the presents, before eventually asking if they could go and see Tweed and Jet in the stables,

"Oh, go on then," Jane said, but put your wellies on and your coats, and wipe your feet before you come in." Bruce and Mark who were just coming down the stairs, thought they had better go with them and take the hurricane lamp as the sky was already beginning to darken. Fiona jumped up and said she would go too. The horses were feeding peacefully pulling on their hay-nets and munching with a dreamy look on their faces as they stood in a bed of clean deep straw. The boys were quick to note that they looked smart as Fiona had clipped them out with a half clip which left thicker hair on their backs to keep them warm while the places where they sweated and couldn't dry off quickly had been clipped to stop them getting a chill.

Fiona stayed and had tea with them all before excusing herself, to go home. "Dad and I will see you tonight at midnight mass."

"Oh, my goodness, I hope I can stay awake," Jane said.

"Oh, you will love it," Fiona said. "It just makes Christmas, it would be nothing without the service. Be sure to come, all of you," she admonished. "Bye." When she had gone, Jane said, "I wouldn't have thought of her as religious."

"Fiona is passionate about all sorts of things. I think I rather love her for it." Vicky said.

They set out at half-past-eleven to go to the service. As they got out of the car, snow was falling gently, lightly covering the path up to the kirk. As they entered, they could see that it was packed but Fiona had been reserving a whole pew for them. John rose and greeted them, kissing Vicky lightly on the cheek, as she sat beside him. Vicky looked around her. The crib, the red-berried holly, the hanging ivy, The lit candles flickering on the altar, the night darkening the stained glass windows behind. They were there to hear again the ancient familiar words which spoke of the humility of despised shepherds, and men of wisdom and learning who were travelling by an unusual star seeking something, which turned out to be a vulnerable baby, with God's Spirit upon him, born in a stable cave, who was destined to proclaim love, peace and servant-hood, to a cruel, blind, indifferent world. On the stroke of midnight they stood to sing, Adeste Fideles,---" Yea, Lord, we greet Thee, born this happy morning----O come, let us adore Him, Christ the Lord." It was Christmas morning, and everybody wished each other, a happy Christmas. John felt moved as she was, and held her close.

The snow was still falling as the boys tried to slide along the path to the car. John, wished them a good night's sleep, before he and Fiona came round for dinner later that day, and off they drove.

"Oh, my goodness, it has been a very long day, I can't wait to get to bed. I hope we haven't got to get up early."

"If I know anything about boys," Vicky said, "they will be our alarm clocks opening their presents at daylight."

"Yea!" The boys shouted waving their arms above their heads. Mark and Jane shooed them off to bed, making them promise to be as quiet as church-mice in the morning.

Fiona and John came late in the afternoon. They came bearing gifts. The grown-ups as yet had not opened their presents unlike the boys who had crept down at dawn to open theirs and were now still absorbed in them as well as each other's. After everyone had had a drink Vicky asked Fiona to give out the presents. The tearing of paper, the oohs and ahhs drawing the interest of the others to admire or laugh. There was perfume and purple tights for Jane. Sweaters, and a fine whisky for the men, books and a jumper for Vicky. Bruce had bought Fiona a silver pen and Fiona had bought Bruce a leather cartridge belt. John had a book about survival from Bruce and a contract for his book. A wrist compass and map holder from Vicky. John slyly handed his present to Vicky last of all so that all eyes were on her when she opened it. The parcel was large and soft. Something which resembled that of a wolf dropped softly from the folds of tissue paper. It was a ¾ length grey fur coat complete with an opulent hood. It was quite beautiful but John had anticipated the unspoken question,

"No, it's not wolf but faux fur, I promise"

"Try it on. Try it on." they all said. Vicky put it on. "It's stunning mum," from Jane.

"You won't be able to wear it here," John said, "because if you do you will definitely frighten the horses." They all laughed, without understanding quite what he meant. Vicky felt a rising panic. What was John going to come out with next, she wondered? Jane's eyebrows had gone up questioningly as she looked over at Mark. Fiona's eyebrows too, as she looked across to Bruce. Unspoken questions arose in their minds. What was going on? What did it all mean?

A card had dropped out from inside Vicky's present and lay on the floor, until Fiona picked it up with all the wrapping paper that lay strewn there, as she helped Vicky to restore order before they had dinner. She glanced at it and read, *'to my dearest Vicky, my alpha-she -wolf-mate. Won't you come with me?* Oh, Father! she thought, embarrassed at what he had written. Quickly she tucked it into the wolf-coat pocket. And then reasoned that you said and did crazy things when you were in love. It was a sort of madness that takes you over, she thought a little miserably.

Around the festive dinner table, talk was mainly about John's forthcoming research with the release of wolves in America. A lot hinged on what conclusions he would draw from it as to whether it could be feasible in parts of Scotland; to see how far the wolves ranged if food became scarce, breeding limitations etc. It was to be a serious scientific study for two years at least. Jane looked across at her mother to see what reaction there was to the length of time he was to be gone. Fiona looked at her father and thought,

Oh, so that's what it's all about, he wants her to go with him, hmm!

Vicky, suddenly busied herself collecting the dinner plates. Bruce was thinking, I hope mum doesn't feel that she has to stay with me and Callum, we can manage now. But how to put it to his mother? Fiona had hinted more than once to him, that her father and his mother were fond of one another. With all the trauma going on his life, he guessed he had been too busy to notice, but now--?

Vicky went out to the kitchen. When she returned with the Christmas pudding alight with brandy, a cheer went up, and the conversation had changed to where they might all go riding to-morrow if the weather allowed.

The next morning as Vicky rode Jet and Callum rode his pony Tweed, over to John's, the others piled into the Land Rover suitably kitted out and drove to Ordie House where they found that Fiona had got a horse a-piece bridled and saddled for Jane and Mark and two ponies ready for the boys to ride. By the time James had made little adjustments to the stirrup lengths for the boys and tightened their girths, Vicky and Callum arrived and so they all set out on a ride together. Bruce and Fiona rode together so that they could look after the three boys. Jane rode with Mark and Vicky and John brought up the rear. He pulled his big bay gelding over closer to Jet and mouthed across to Vicky,

"Will you marry me?" Jet, ever a flighty thoroughbred mare laid her ears back at the closeness of the bay horse and screamed a high-pitched whinny at him before plunging away. "Oh, I'm sorry Vicky." he said mortified as she struggled to regain her seat and control the mare, who was now thoroughly spooked and wanted to plunge into a headlong gallop. She calmed the mare down and by this time they had dropped behind. She gave John, what could only be described as a 'look,' before trotting on to catch the others up.

They had decided previously to ride Vicky's circular route which would be the lane intersecting John's estate, a trot or canter through woodland, to where a track followed a stream for a couple of miles. Crossing that, they climbed the lower slopes around the side of a mountain before reaching 'the Croft' to rest the horses, stretch their legs while Vicky made them a hot cup of chocolate, and see whether or not anyone wanted to drop out. The snow was still on the tops of the mountains giving them a grandeur as the grey rock thrust through the snow, but the temperature had warmed up slightly melting the snow at ground level. It was exhilarating Vicky thought, after all that feasting and lounging around the fire, to be outside on this fresh dry day. For Jane who had not ridden for many years since she was a girl, she loved it, but knew that she would need a long hot soak in a bath before the party tonight that was to be held at Ordie House, where there was to be invited guests, music and dancing and a buffet meal. It was turning out to be a memorable Christmas, but first they had to ride back. Vicky and Callum had completed the circle, having already ridden to John's, and decided they would drop out to feed and bed the horses down, before they prepared a light tea, so that they would all have time to use the bathroom and shower and change for the party.

"Vicky called after John, "See you tonight, John." As he rode back with the others he pondered on this ambivalent message. Could it be that she was going to give him his answer tonight?

To Vicky, Christmas had been a wonderfully happy family time, the intermingling of both families had been harmonious and great fun. Fiona had been loving and helpful. The boys adored her. Bruce was coming out of his dark time and seemed happier. She had found herself falling under John's spell again and loving him. Her mistrust had gone with the sheer normality of their days together.

* * *

The hall was festooned with holly and bunches of mistletoe A small orchestra played. John greeted them wearing the Highland evening dress with the kilt, as were most of the men there. He took them through into an ante-room to take their coats off, Vicky was wearing John's present to her and he smiled when he saw her and raised his eyebrows questioningly at her. As she slipped her wolf-coat off, she was wearing a long dark blue velvet dress with Venetian glass beads, She looked very elegant. Jane wore a little black dress, showing her long legs in purple tights and stiletto heels, her hair coiled back in the nape of her neck. Bruce and Mark wore evening dress, the boys smart in crisp white shirts and ties and long trousers. Fiona came bustling in looking beautiful with her golden Pre-Raphaelite hair spilling around her head and shoulders, complementing a pale sea-green off-the-shoulder floating chiffon dress, looking so very feminine, which seemed to belie her very strong character. She took them off into the ballroom. John waylaid Vicky and took her off into one of the rooms where they could be alone. He put his arms around her and kissed her gently, then held her from him and told her how beautiful she looked. His eyes were so warm with love for her that she felt herself melt into him as they kissed passionately.

"Now, will you marry me?"

"Yes." she said simply. He caught hold of her hand, "You are not wearing the ring tonight?" She blushed, "No," she murmured.

"Then wear this for me tonight, my darling," he said opening a little box.

"Close your eyes and give me your hand." She felt him slip a ring on her finger. She looked down and gasped and looked up at him,

"You,------ bought it,----but how did you know?"

"Ah, I am not the only one who keeps secrets, and tells lies." He smiled, "I have my spies, but please don't lose it again Ma'am." She laughed, but felt like weeping, "I promise I won't." and kissed him.

"I love you John, and will be honoured to be your wife."

"Yes, yes, but will you come and live in a shack with me?" She gave a little mock howl, "I wouldn't miss it for the world."

"Where has mother disappeared to?" Jane fussed and then saw them suddenly appear holding hands together. John raised his voice for an announcement. The hall suddenly fell silent. John smiled,

"My dear friends, it gives me much happiness to introduce you to my fiancee, Vicky. We are to be married shortly before we leave for America." There was much clapping and murmurs of approval. John beckoned Jane and Mark and their boys over, as well as Bruce and Callum to introduce them as his new family, not forgetting his lovely daughter, Fiona. James and Marian were scurrying around the guests with trays carrying glasses of champagne for a toast. They raised their glasses to John and Vicky. Too late as they saw all three boys down the champagne. "Oh, well," Jane shrugged as she looked at Mark. "Let's keep our eye on them."

John escorted Vicky around his guests introducing her personally. At last when Jane kissed her and congratulated them, she asked to see her mother's engagement ring, and was too non-plussed for any words. Fiona commented on how unusual it was and Bruce was desperately embarrassed as it dawned on him that it was John's money that had bailed him out. Fiona went over to Bruce and linked her arm through his,

"I'm so happy for them, aren't you?" she asked him, "Please say you are." She didn't wait for him to answer, "What does this make our relationship?"

"Goodness knows." he laughed. And realized in that very moment that she loved him. He looked closely at her as she said,

"Would you be my step-brother? And as if still pursuing the thought, "that wouldn't make it incestuous, would it?"

"Only if you loved me," he teased, frowning fiercely at her. She turned on her heel and walked away from him, hiding the tears in her eyes. He wanted to go after her but there were too many eyes watching. His solicitor, Peter Duncan was here. So was Lord and Lady Ross, where he sometimes used their land for shooting parties. There was enough suspicion on him without bringing Fiona into it.

The dancing ended with a rumbustious Gay Gordons before the Last Waltz, where John and Vicky started the dance waltzing dreamily together with her head against his chest. Gradually they were joined by others, then Mark and Jane, Bruce asked Fiona to dance with him.

It was very late as they saw their last guests out. John was so happy he was reluctant to let Vicky out of his sight.

Jane promised that she would ride out with Fiona and the boys if they wanted to, in the morning. They kissed and said their good nights and bundled the children into the car. It had been the most splendid night. Jane in spite of herself was truly happy for her mother. They were so obviously right for each other. She was a different woman now, no longer facing a lonely future. How could she deny her her happiness. Mark was relieved that Jane had come to this conclusion. He thought John was a thoroughly nice man. He hoped now that Jane would put moving house out of her mind. He liked it where they were, and what was more to the point, they could afford it.

Bruce's thoughts were in turmoil. His mother had sold the ring to save him. Now, his mother had the ring back and he had John's money. He decided there was nothing he could do about reparation to John at the moment. Only time would tell. He hoped John's books were going to become best-sellers, He was grateful but somewhat embarrassed.

Mark and Bruce excused themselves and said they were going to bed. Vicky and Jane stayed up for awhile, still excited by the events of the evening and wanting to talk them over together.

"When do you fly off together," Jane asked.

"The end of the week." Jane gasped, "--and you're getting married?"

"Yes, I've got some serious shopping to do."

"I'll say you have."

"We are getting married by special license because of the timescale. John is arranging it."

"You are full of surprises mother!" Jane said,"

*   *   *

163

That night a wind sprang up and became quite violent as it developed into gale force. It woke Bruce up as he heard the old farmhouse creak as the wind whistled through any little crack. He heard what sounded like a metal bucket rolling around outside and wondered what damage would confront him in the morning.

Thankfully, next morning, the wind had died down. Bruce was out examining the sheds and barns to see if there was any damage as John called for Vicky to go off together to make their arrangements. Bruce and Mark were going on a shoot and the boys begged to be taken too. Fiona rode down on her horse and helped Jane saddle up Jet for their ride together. As they rode off, Jane said, "I am so enjoying riding again. All the time that I was training seriously and then my time as a dancer, it was denied me. It develops the wrong muscles," she explained. "Although I think it is probably good for turnout."

"Well, you can ride every day now until you go back," Fiona said, "I just love it too. How long can you stay for?"

"Ah, well, that's just it. We were going home in a couple of days but now there is a marriage and then they are flying off to America, so we ought to stay and see them wed and then wave them off. It has all been such a surprise. How do you feel about it, Fiona?"

"I think it is great, I really love your mum, and Dad was so miserable before---" her voice trailed off. "I do wonder who will look after Callum though, when your mum goes"

"There are ways around this," Jane said," Bruce could get a housekeeper to live in, or Callum could come back with us and board at the boys school with them and he could come back for half-term and holidays."

"Umm?----- Come on let's have a gallop." Fiona said changing the subject. They gave the horses their heads, and they stretched out their necks and galloped like race-horses. They pulled them up just as they came to the little lane crossing Ordie House estate and walked the horses sedately along the tarmac. Jane was out of breath after the exhilaration of the gallop and slightly ahead as she approaching the barn on the side of the lane. "Oh look!" She said to Fiona. "The wind last night has made all those bales of straw fall down." Wisps of straw was strewn all over the lane blowing about in the wind. Then to her surprise she saw that the fallen bales had exposed part of a very old khaki coloured Land Rover.---Who on earth would bury a Land Rover under bales of dirty looking straw in a barn? she thought. And then it came to her in a blinding flash-----and her heart raced at the thought. Fiona had made no comment except to say that she would get James to clear it up. Jane had not stopped or pulled her horse up and they had passed the barn and were now near Ordie House.

"Come in for a coffee," Fiona invited. Jane ostensibly looked at her watch, "Not this time, thank you, Fiona, I had better get back. I'll be okay, I can remember the way."

"Are you sure?"

"Yes, I'll be fine, thank you."

Fiona stood and watched her go thoughtfully, before turning her horse into the stables. As Jane rode back she deliberated with herself. She couldn't possibly tell her mother or John, Fiona was his little girl. She couldn't tell Bruce. It would tear him apart. She would tell Mark. He would know what to do. He was always so sensible. When she got back to the house everybody was out still. She gave Jet a brush down, put her night rug on, filled her hay net and put a pan of nuts in her bowl. Tweed was left looking expectantly over the door of his stable, so she thought that she had better feed him too. Doing these simple tasks helped to calm her frazzled nerves.

Once in the house she showered and changed. It was getting dark as Bruce and Mark returned with the boys, who were full of the good time they had had as beaters. Jane thought how they would have enjoyed hollering their heads off to frighten the pheasants' and get them to take flight, without realizing that their fate was doomed as they flew in the direction of the waiting guns. They had brought several brace of pheasant back with them which they proceeded to hang up in the old wash house, next to the larder.

"Had a good day with Fiona?" Bruce asked.

"Yes, fine thanks."

"How does she feel about the marriage?"

"She's happy with it, more worried about how you will cope having Callum, without mum's help."

"We'll manage." he said.

Mark went upstairs to shower and change. Jane followed him up, shut their bedroom door, to stop Bruce or the boys from overhearing what she had to tell Mark. "What do you think?" she asked him when she had told him about the bales of straw that had been hiding an old Land Rover.

"If you are wise, you will forget it," he said shortly and went and turned the shower on. She walked downstairs slowly. Obviously Mark was not taking this seriously. Should she go to the police, she wondered? Just then her mother walked in with John. For all the world she looked like the cat who had stolen the cream, Jane thought a little sourly in her worried state. Vicky linked her arm through John's as she announced they were to be married at Ordie House tomorrow morning at eleven.

"What are you going to wear?" Jane asked open-mouthed.

"We've done our shopping." she smiled up at John,

"But I haven't." Jane yelped, "What am I going to wear?"

*   *   *

Ordie House was still garlanded with holly, mistletoe and arum lilies. A log fire blazed in the baronial hearth. There were only the family there, and Marian and James and the Minister. Jane wore her little black number she had worn at the party and borrowed a cream stole from her mother. Fiona too, wore the sea-green chiffon dress she had on the other night. John was resplendent in his Highland evening dress, as he stood waiting for his bride flanked by Mark.

Vidor's organ Toccata was playing as Vicky entered the room wearing the long dark blue velvet dress, with the Venetian glass beads. It all seemed very appropriate in the rather grand setting. Bruce, smart in evening dress led his mother to the waiting groom, where they exchanged their vows, and rings and were declared man and wife. They turned to each other and kissed. A young girl came in with drinks and Marian and James retreated to the kitchen to lay out the wedding breakfast, while the couple signed the register. Jane accosted her mother, "I thought you told us, last night that you had gone shopping for an outfit?"

"Vicky laughed, "Yes, we did. Outfits for the outback." Jane was not amused.

The informality of it just being family, showed in Fiona's playfulness with the boys, and a certain familiarity with Bruce as she brushed some crumbs off his lapel. All this was worryingly obvious to Jane. She expected Fiona to be a little distant with her, but she wasn't at all, quite the opposite as she asked her when they would ride out again. Jane thought that she should have asked her outright at the time why a Land Rover was buried under bales of straw in their barn? As she observed her, she pondered whether she thought Fiona was capable of murder. Her mother suddenly broke into her dark thoughts by asking her to be sure to feed the horses as she wouldn't be returning to The Croft until the next day, "Fiona tells me you will be riding with her tomorrow morning, so call in for a coffee with me and John, will you? You can stable the mare here."

"Alright," Jane said, thinking that it would give her a chance to look at the barn again, and maybe pluck up courage to ask Fiona about the hidden vehicle.

It seemed strange when their mother didn't return home with them, and then Fiona asked whether anyone would mind her coming to stay the night with them. Bruce said she was welcome. All the boys thought that it was a wonderful idea. Jane thought that she could understand why Fiona didn't want to play gooseberry on John and Vicky's wedding night and agreed with Bruce. Fiona helped her feed, water and bed down the horses for the night.

*   *   *

Bruce had been asleep when he suddenly became aware that someone was getting into bed with him. He guessed it was Callum who would sometimes do this, and then, as he put out an arm to enfold him, was electrified by the knowledge that it wasn't Callum but Fiona who had slipped into his bed. He lay there faking sleep, every nerve alert, wondering what he should say or do. She neither spoke nor touched him, but seemed to have curled up with her back to him and just gone to sleep by the sound of her steady breathing. He was afraid to move in case he disturbed her but at some time he must have dropped off and when he awoke she was gone. He shook his head. Did he dream this?

Downstairs, Mark informed Bruce that it was just them for breakfast, as Jane and Fiona had gone for an early ride together. The boys had gone for a walk up to the post-box, taking Hamish the dog with them.

Because Fiona's horse was up at Ordie House, she had asked Callum if she could ride Tweed to accompany Jane who would be riding Jet.

"Of course," for Fiona, he would have agreed to anything. Fiona was as much at home riding the Highland pony as she was on her big hunter.

"Ponies are more fun," she said to Jane, "far more adaptable than any horse. You can ask them to go anywhere or do anything and they will. Far more hardy too." She started to show off on Tweed, popping him over logs and ditches, while Jane rode Jet sedately around all the obstacles that Tweed was flying over. As they approached the familiar lane with the barn on the side of it. Jane noticed that all the mouldy looking old bales of hay and straw had been put back again, piled high and perhaps still hiding the old Land Rover from view again.

"Someone's been busy," she said to Fiona.

"Yes, I expect James did it, terrible storm wasn't it?" Jane took a big breath and tried to sound casual as they walked the horses past. "Why is that old Land Rover buried under it?"

"Oh, I expect it conked out years ago, when there were no scrap-yards and people used to leave their old cars and tractors all over the countryside. Daddy would never do that and I expect that is why it was buried a long time ago." *Mmm,--- plausible, Jane thought, but she had had time to think of a credible answer.* They stabled Jet and Tweed and went to the house. Vicky and John welcomed them both. Jane kissed her mother,

"Good morning Mrs Brown," she said with a smile. Marian brought in the coffee. And Jane watched 'madam' pour.

"This time tomorrow mum, we shall be waving you off at the airport, and then we shall be off too. We have all had a wonderful time, and I have gained a sister," she said, throwing an affectionate arm around Fiona.

"We shall look after her John when she is in London, so don't worry about her."

"Thank you, Jane.

"I'll be down later to pack." Vicky said, as she strolled arm in arm with John over to the stables with them, and watched them ride off with some amusement to see Fiona on Tweed, pretending to be a cossack galloping madly past them, riding at a dangerous angle to the ground.

When they arrived back, Bruce offered to run Fiona home. Jane said quickly, "Oh, it's our last night here. Would you prefer to stay with us, Fiona.

"Yes, thank you, I would," and so it was settled. After a meal together, and the boys had gone to bed Mark and Jane excused themselves to go and pack for their flight home tomorrow.

When they were alone Bruce said to Fiona, "What was all that about, last night?" Her ice-blue eyes widened as she looked up at him with surprise and then looked down as she said, "I didn't think you knew." and actually blushed. "You see," she explained, "everybody had someone---- except you and me.----- I was lonely------I just wanted to lie beside you." He smiled down at her, "Oh, Fiona, I'm in enough trouble as it is---"

"I know, I'm sorry."

"Don't be sorry, I'm sorry." He raised his hands in a helpless gesture and she suddenly flung herself at him, arms around him, head buried in his chest. She mumbled, "I love you so much, Bruce." It was such a spontaneous gesture of affection that his arms that had been hanging helplessly by his side automatically went around her. Fiona thought, if only she could stay like this for ever. They sprang apart as Jane entered the room. She knew at once that something had happened between them as she looked from one to the other.

"Oh, I er," she started uncertainly, "I just came down to ask you Fiona, whether you would like to come back to London with us tomorrow, if we can get an extra ticket?"

"No thank you Jane, it would be too early for me. I shall have the house to myself to revise in and then I shall go back by train later this month.

Bruce lay awake wondering if Fiona would come to him again, and whether he should order her to return to her bed if she did. He doubted truthfully if he would take such a high moral stand with her, but if he didn't, wasn't he letting her father down when he obviously trusted him to do the right thing by his daughter? He was an experienced man, with the suspicion of murder hanging over him. She was a young girl, no doubt infatuated with him. Sleep eventually got the better of him and he didn't wake until he felt the restriction of an arm flung across his chest. It was Fiona. Gently he tried removing her arm, but as she stirred in her sleep, her grasp tightened around him. Once again he couldn't move. "Fiona," he said quietly, but firmly. She stirred and turned over and went to sleep. Bruce nearly burst out laughing. What a ludicrous situation! No one would ever believe the sheer innocence of it. But this time she stayed in his bed until morning. When he awoke he could hear the children about, and shook her awake. She was totally unrepentant and giggled at his embarrassment as he worried that Jane might come in with a cup of tea. She got up, put her dressing gown on, planted a kiss on his lips, and walked out of his bedroom regardless of who might see, only to come back a few minutes later with two cups of tea.

CHAPTER SEVENTEEN

Bruce, drove his sister, Mark and the boys to the airport while James drove Fiona, Vicky and John. There were hugs and kisses all round, before John and Vicky finally went beyond passport control and out of sight. They were off on their big adventure, promising to keep in touch when they could. They all scrambled to a viewing place where they saw them board the plane and waved madly hoping they could be seen until the plane taxied out of sight.

"Let's go and have a coffee before we go our separate ways," Jane suggested, looking at her watch. There was time before their flight, and she felt the reality of the anti-climax of the sobering thought that they and Fiona, wouldn't be seeing their respective parent again for two years. As they drank their coffee, Jane fussed over Bruce telling him that it would never be any trouble for them to have Callum should any difficulty arise and to keep in touch. "You haven't heard from the police again?" she asked Bruce.

"Well yes, I have. I rang Detective Mike Greig to ask if I could go ahead and sell Lindsay's flat. He said I could. I asked him if there had been any developments and he said that the paintwork from the vehicle which had been in collision with Lindsay's car making it swerve into the ditch, was from a very old Fifties Land Rover with khaki paintwork, but they still hadn't found it." Jane and Mark's eyes met as she choked on the last mouthful of coffee. Oh, my Goodness, it really is true! Jane thought.

"We have one like that." Fiona said cooly.

"Come on, let's get going," Mark said. Callum said goodbye to his cousins, kissed his aunt and shook hands with Mark. Bruce thanked them for coming and said that he would keep in touch. Fiona said, "I'll come and see you when I'm at Uni." and threw her arms around Jane as she kissed her.

Jane stood frozen in horror as she watched her brother walk away with Callum between him and Fiona, holding their hands. For all the world an idyllic little family picture. She grasped Mark's arm, a worried question about to spring from her lips,

"Not now Jane. The boys,--" he warned quietly tight lipped.

"But, it's my brother!"

"Yes, and it is also the entire family that is going to be drawn into it. Forget it, Jane!" said Mark tersely. "Forget you ever saw it, for God's sake!"

*   *   *

As Vicky sat back on her seat in the plane, a little smile hovered over her face as she thought about her marriage to John. Somehow it all seemed so miraculous that they were now actually man and wife when they had so nearly parted over Fiona, of all people, who had been so loving to her lately. John had gone to such lengths to part them to protect Fiona from any implied scandal by her association with her family.

She thought back to their conversation. It was all a bit of a muddle now, in her mind. So much had happened since. What had he said---that he couldn't tell her---couldn't divulge whatever it was to her. Then he had told her that it was to do with Fiona---and that he had thought the unimaginable about his own daughter, but then that she had convinced him that she hadn't anything to do with the accident. And although he said he believed her utterly, they had disappeared to London because he was afraid for her. She frowned. Somehow she hadn't quite resolved this in her mind. Should she ask him again to explain it again. The plane started to taxi down the runway as John buckled himself into the seat beside her. He took hold of her hand and smiled at her with pure happiness. "Happy, my darling, Mrs Brown?"

"Very, Mr Brown" she said smiling. How long is the flight?"

"Eight long hours I'm afraid, and then another flight in the morning." He opened a book that he had bought at the airport and started to read. She lay her head back and tried to sleep. Obviously this was not the right time to start asking questions. She found herself unconsciously twisting the ring on her little finger. She looked at it and wondered idly at the part it might have played in Queen Victoria's life when she had fallen in love with her John Brown? It was an impossible love affair, doomed from the start and ending in ignominy of drunkenness for him, that some say he was trapped into, by the family who disapproved of the part he played in the Queen's affections. The Queen did not speak to John again for four years until he lay on his death-bed. Whereupon she became prostrate with grief at his death. And when she herself died years later, her trusted doctor carried out her last wishes concealing a lock of John Brown's hair with her in the coffin. The family then burnt diaries and anything else that appertained to her close association.

What a strange twist of fate that this little ring was now the token and fulfilment of their love affair. She didn't want any shadow to be cast over their love. She would forget the uncertainties that had come into her mind. They loved each other and that was all that mattered. She closed her eyes and settled back.

After the long flight a taxi took them to their hotel where she flopped into bed. John went down to the bar to get a drink. When he came to bed she was asleep. In the morning, she heard her mobile ringing. John was in the shower. It was Jane. She frowned as she listened, then she laughed. "No, you are mistaken, surely.----What? ---Oh dear, my mobile is breaking up. I can't hear you----I forgot to charge it last night. Have to go. We have a plane to catch. Bye darling."

"Who was that?" John asked emerging from the shower.

"It was Jane, just a brief call."

"Everything alright?" She started to say "Yes, fine. Well,--- I'm not sure. It was all a bit garbled and my mobile started to pack up."

He looked at his watch "You'd better hurry up and get in that shower, or we'll miss the plane, he warned."

*　　*　　*

Mark glanced up from reading the Sunday Times as Jane entered the sitting room looking pensive. "Anything the matter?" he asked.

"I just rang mother."

"Where are they?"

"About to catch their plane out West.----- I told her about our suspicions---"

"Oh Jane, I told you not to stir things up," he said annoyed. "What did she say?"

"That I must be mistaken. Then her mobile started to break up. She had to go. They had another flight to catch. End of conversation."

"Well, there you are, perhaps there really is nothing to worry about."

"I'm not convinced." she said. "I think I ought to ring Bruce. He is my brother and could be in a very dangerous position," she reasoned. "He ought to know." Mark groaned, "Oh Jane, I hope you know what you are doing."

*   *   *

Bruce answered the phone, "Hello Sis?" he sounded pleased, almost jovial. Jane carefully started to launch into her suspicions, when Bruce stopped her by cutting across her with the news that Morag, Graham's wife had been arrested. She has confessed. We are so relieved that this terrible business is over and we can all now get on with our lives."

"Oh!--- Oh, thank God Bruce. I have been so concerned about you---- forgive me for thinking that it could have been Fiona, but I could see how much she loved you and was hurt for you and Callum. I just wondered whether---she's such an impulsive girl---" Her voice trailed off in embarrassment. "Please don't tell her, will you? I think she is a great girl."

"No, I won't tell her." he sounded a little bemused. "wondering what on earth she had been rambling about. "I too think she's a great girl. In fact, that's why I love her."

"But how did the police find the Land Rover?" Jane persisted.

"They haven't., That's the thing. Morag confessed to causing the accident but so far she wont tell them what she has done with the Land Rover. It's a great shame, because I liked her, and she was the other wronged partner too."

Jane sat and thought about the telephone call to her brother. There were only the three of them who knew where the offending Land Rover was hidden;herself, Fiona, and Morag. Morag had had the courage to confess, but was obviously protecting Fiona who had hidden it for her. Bruce was now vindicated. So, what good would it do if she pursued this? She knew what Mark would say. No, what good would it do?

When John answered his mobile and it was Fiona, Vicky went to leave him to have some privacy with his daughter, but he caught hold of her and drew her close to himself. She saw that as he listened, relief flooded his face, before he thanked Fiona for phoning, and telling her how much he loved her. He turned to Vicky and told her of Morag's confession and arrest..

"Oh, thank God. I'm so relieved for Bruce, but I am saddened that it was Morag and to think what jealousy can lead people to do," as she remembered the friendship that had once been between Morag and Lindsay.

"My darling Vicky, we can let go of all the anxiety, suspicions, the agony I put you through. It's all over. Today is a new day. When I think how this could have destroyed us-----" Tears rose in his eyes and trickled down his face and in a broken voice he said, "I didn't believe her Vicky, I hoped that it wasn't true, but I didn't quite believe her. That is so terrible of me---her father," he sobbed as he shook his head. This is what I couldn't bring myself to tell you. You see, I saw her the next day in Morag's Land Rover up at Ordie House and I wondered why?" Later, when the news had circulated about Lindsays death I asked Fiona about it, she told me that Morag had wanted some hay for her horses and Fiona took her to the barn to get some for her. Vicky put her arms around him and they clung together. She kissed him tenderly and tasted his bitter salt tears and thought to herself that he was not the only one to have thought the unimaginable about dear impetuous Fiona.

"By he way, that's not all the news." he said, smiling at her.

"What, what is it?"

"They love each other---

"Who?"

"Fiona and Bruce",

"I could have told you that." she laughed. He looked into her eyes, "Oh, Mrs Vicky Brown, I love you."

"Oh, John Brown, I love you too."

*　　*　　*

She touched the ring with its Celtic intertwining love knots and thought that it was not going to be a ring of tragedy for them after all. The ring had been redeemed after years of lying in a cold loch and redeemed yet again when it was auctioned and bought by John and their love too had been redeemed again through all the stress and trauma of their family. There were no secrets now. It was a new beginning for them all.

*　　*　　*

Bruce was reading the report of Morag's confession to Fiona, from the local paper. It says that Morag never intended to harm Lindsay, just to scare her but they had unfortunately hit each other. She was so busy trying to control the skid from the impact that by the time she had it under control she was out of sight of Lindsay's car and didn't know that it had overturned into the culvert and that they had drowned. She got rid of the Land Rover, but refuses to tell the police what she did with it. What do you think about that?" he asked Fiona, as they sat eating breakfast together. "She will get a longer sentence for hiding evidence." he added. "And of course if someone has disposed of it for her, then they too will become an accessory after the fact." Fiona looked up, "Is that so?" she asked and carried on spreading her toast with marmalade, "Poor Morag," she said quietly, remembering a distraught Morag tumbling out of the dented Land Rover saying, "Have you heard the news about Lindsay?"-----Fiona had nodded, and Morag carried on hysterically "Her car was in collision with the Land Rover--- but I didn't mean to kill her—seeing her suddenly made me swerve at her----in that moment I just meant to----- to frighten her----to show her that she had ruined my life too—and I hated her--- but I didn't mean to kill her," she had sobbed. When I looked back the car had gone out of sight and I assumed that she had driven on---and I just drove on back home---I didn't know until today what had happened. I don't know what to do? I am appalled" and she covered her face with her hands." Fiona had pushed her into the passenger seat and had climbed into the driving seat of the Land Rover. "Let's get away from the house," she had said, as she started the engine and drove round to where the barns stood beside the lane. There, she had easily hidden the offending vehicle under a pile of old straw. "Remember, you came to me for some bales of hay for your horses" she had instructed Morag as she had driven her home in her car.

"I must ring Father and Vicky and tell them that you are finally vindicated." Fiona said, smiling up at Bruce. "I knew you would be."

EPILOGUE

OSBORNE HOUSE,
ISLE of WIGHT 1901

The Queen lay dying. Her voice was weak as she constantly rambled and muttered about a lost ring. She touched her hand over and over again as she muttered. "I've lost it.------Do you know where it is?" she implored those seated at her bedside, Where is my ring? Get me my ring."

A hundred and forty odd years would pass before the ring was found and amazingly now graced the hand of another Victoria, the wife of John Brown!

Lightning Source UK Ltd.
Milton Keynes UK
UKOW03f1806120914

238467UK00001B/16/P